Eggnog & Candy Canes

EGGNOG AND CANDY CANES

A BLUEBERRY SPRINGS CHRISTMAS NOVELLA

JEAN ORAM

Eggnog and Candy Canes
A Blueberry Springs Christmas Novella (Book 3) © 2014
Jean Oram

Cover design by Najla Qamber Media & Designs

Complete cataloguing information available online or upon request.

Oram, Jean.

Eggnog and Candy Canes: A Blueberry Springs Christmas Novella / Jean Oram.—2nd. ed.

ISBN 978-1-928198-97-0, 978-1-928198-07-9 (paperback)

Ebook ISBN 978-1-928198-06-2

Summary: When a nurse and doctor butt heads on Christmas Eve in the Blueberry Springs hospital, it is a family emergency while being snowed in that brings them together and allows them to finally see eye to eye.

Second Oram Productions Edition: May 2020

To Alayna Dickerson for the eggnog. (I'm sorry.)

To my Fan Girls (Jeansters) for saying, "Heck ya! Nash has to come back—and get together with Katie!"

This book would not have written itself without the encouragement and writing sprints with fellow author Mallory Crowe. Thanks girl!

I'd also like to give thanks to my critiquers, helping hands, editors, and proofreaders: Evelyn Adams, Tiesha Brunson, Jemi Fraser, Anne Welch, Jenn Gallagher, Margaret Carney, Erin Dixon, and Emily Kirkpatrick. Thank you for helping me put my best foot forward.

To my readers—may you get what you want for the holidays.

There was only one way to make the already dreaded holiday season worse.

And thanks to nurse Katie Reiter's cousin, the staffing director of the Blueberry Springs hospital--a man Katie had believed to be on her side when he'd loaded her schedule with requested shifts blanketing December 24 to 26--it was happening.

Nash Leham, her arch nemesis and biggest rival for the title of the Most Organized and Detail-oriented Staff Member, was back.

"Hello, Katie." Nash's blue eyes sized her up and she felt as though they were delving into her soul in a way she'd forgotten was possible. And seeing a lot more than she allowed most to see.

She scooted behind the nurses' station. "Hello, Dr. Leham," she said curtly, before mentally slapping herself for forgetting their old game. She'd meant to be cool and aloof, calling him "Doctor," a title that was much too formal for Blueberry Springs, instead of giving him what he wanted--authority. Although that game was from back when he'd been engaged to her best friend, now sister-in-law. Back before he'd become the jilted groom, and returned to his natural habitat--the city. And now Katie had just handed Mr. Alpha Top Dog a one-up by calling him Dr. Leham instead of Nash.

Maybe she could blame the holiday season for softening her edges.

Or maybe she needed to pull herself together.

"Welcome back." She quickly rearranged files, hiding her *In Style* and French fashion magazines, and generally attempting to appear completely organized. Being bare-bones staff for Christmas Eve, Katie had taken the rare luxury of spreading out the files she was working on. People said that Nash had changed after Beth dumped him, but there were only so many ways a guy like him would change, and Katie was pretty sure he was still capable of his "let's keep our patients safe by staying organized" lectures.

"Looking for double pay to afford that perfect life and snappy style of yours?" she asked. Okay, so she was being a bit of a you-know-what, but they hadn't exactly gotten along in the past and she might as well remind him that she wasn't about to fawn over him like the other nurses used to.

And yeah, her conscience was reminding her that they'd done good work together and that he was actually a decent guy who had tried to do well by her friend, but it hadn't worked out. Beth was over it; Katie should be, too.

Except she was pretty sure that if she softened her stance in their mini war he would go in for the proverbial kill. The man had so many rules and regulations memorized, as well as that fat stick shoved so far up his hiney it was a miracle he could bend over to tie his polished Oxfords. She had taken these extra holiday shifts to chill out and avoid situations that would make her head explode, thank you very much. And here he was, making her life miserable.

"You like my style?" Nash asked, eyes narrowed.

Yes. Now go away. Forever.

"Too pretentious."

In truth, she loved the fact that Nash never wore stained, worn-out or disheveled attire. He exuded classy confidence and his blond hair was always perfect. She'd hated his old Blueberry Springs condo for only one reason: she'd wanted it to be hers. It had been a homey blend of comfort, style, and modern simplicity. In other words, it had stood for everything Katie didn't have in her life.

"Above my station?" he asked.

"Not exactly." She smoothed her ponytail. "Just trying to be bigger and better than everyone else. As usual."

He leaned against the counter and whispered in a low, suggestive voice that sent shivers through her soul, "Maybe I *am* bigger and better than everyone else, Katie Reiter."

Okay, that was a different side of Nash. Definitely. She needed to close her mouth and stop imagining him taking her in the little storage closet just down the hall, her name on his lips as he…

Oh, wow. This whole being on the rebound after being dumped by one's long-term boyfriend was messing with her brain. That's what it had to be. Not…lust. Not for Nash.

Yuck.

He grinned, as if knowing the effect he was having, and patted the counter's worn surface. "I'm back for two days."

"Is it day two?" she asked hopefully. The sooner he was out of here the better.

Nash's serious blue eyes took her in. She smoothed her ponytail again and stood a tad taller, matching his height. Hm. She could have sworn she was taller than he was.

"Day one. Hour one." He straightened his crisp, white doctor's coat. "Filling in. Being a nice guy. All that. It is possible, you know."

"How did I not know you were coming? I must have missed the hounds of hell howling to announce your imminent arrival."

"Well, Miss Head Nurse, I know this is may be news to you, so

I'll break it to you gently. The gist of it is you don't know everything."

What. A. Jerk.

"I didn't miss you one iota."

His eyes darkened with what she could have sworn was disappointment, if it had been pretty much anyone other than Nash.

They stared at each other in silence and Katie wondered if he'd heard about the party she'd held when he'd finally returned to the city to resume his oh-so-amazing career somewhere not filled with backward, casual, unprofessional hicks. Old anger stirred as she thought of his consummate professional attitude and let's-make-things-better, gung-ho persona.

In other words, it had been nice having him gone. Really nice.

"You look well," he said. "Is Will treating you right?"

"Well, he dumped me, so yes. I suppose from your viewpoint, he is treating me right." Go figure that the one time Nash deigned to ask about her life it was to poke a finger in the festering sore of being dumped when she'd been expecting an engagement ring.

Men. So typically unreliable.

Nash's expression closed and Katie resisted the urge to ask about his own love life. Not because she wanted to know--it was Nash, after all. But because *that* would be a sore worth poking. It would also likely be the very definition of awkward, seeing as, one, her brother was the reason Nash wasn't happily married to her best friend. And two, her best friend had dumped him. For her brother. Full circle. A whole big tangled ball of awkward.

Plus, add in the whole yay-he-left-town party thing.

"We have a suture in ER room three," Nash said quietly.

He seemed bothered by her banter. Where was his usual spunk? His volley back over the net? That knowing smirk that used to drive her mad and make her vow to get further under his skin next time?

He couldn't leave her hanging here as the big bad, snippy wolf, could he?

Well, he was Nash, so yes he could.

But maybe he really had changed. Which would mean she'd have to be nice.

Boo. Hiss. That wasn't going to happen. Him playing Mr. Nice Guy was probably a game aimed at getting back at her for decorating his Beemer with streamers when he'd left town.

"Amy is dispensing meds, so you're on." He turned, glancing over his shoulder expectantly when she didn't fall into step behind him like the perfect little nurse she was supposed to be.

She was starting to really despise nursing. Even more than usual.

"Of course," she muttered, hanging back enough to prove that they were most definitely *not* walking together.

Approaching room three, where town gossip and newspaper reporter Liz Moss-Brady was apparently waiting for them, Nash turned, trapping Katie unexpectedly in a small, blaringly white corner. His eyes were serious and oh so blue. She froze, not knowing what to expect.

Hot diggedy, he smelled good. The same cologne as her brother, she'd guess, except on Nash it smelled…sexy. Definitely not an innocent scent. It was as though someone had taken all the testosterone in the world, all the sexiness and…*no.*

This was Nash. Her supervisor for the next two days.

She inhaled involuntarily. Yep, totally different than on her brother. On Nash, the scent was as though Daniel Craig and Ryan Gosling had morphed into one megasexy being that contained their appeal as well as the pull of a dreamy accent such as Pierce Brosnan's and the primal ferocity of Wolverine. All wrapped into one man. One scent.

Completely dangerous.

And her body had noticed. Was definitely reacting. Knees weak and jelly-like. Pulse throbbing. Clammy anticipation swinging through her nerve endings. Check, check, checkity-check. Her body was gearing up in a way that was similar to the primal "give it to me'" call of the wild. If she were a rhesus monkey, her butt cheeks would be a shocking red right now.

Ew. Not a sexy thought. And now she'd never be able to inhale around her brother without feeling incredibly uncomfortable.

Great. Thanks a lot, Nash Leham. You big monkey bottom.

"Katie," Nash said in his serious-doctor-melodrama voice. "Can we just drop it?"

"Drop what?" She glanced at his hands. So perfect. Clean. Strong. Deft. No wonder he was a good doctor, a good surgeon and likely a very good lover.

She returned her attention to his face so fast she just about gave herself vertigo. What was her problem today? Unused hormones lingering around, not realizing that having been dumped she simply didn't need them messing with her? Because it had been two simple, carefree weeks and the hormones should just go away and never come back until she said it was safe.

Right now? Not safe.

"This." He pointed to her chest, then his own. "Whatever invisible thing we've been fighting, let's drop it and enjoy the next couple of days."

Katie tried to form words.

He smiled as though confiding in her, and her knees weakened again. "We're a good team, Katie. One of the best. Let's rock it out of the park."

They *were* a good team. Even though they were always fighting and trying to one-up and cut each other off. Well, no… that was mostly just her. Trying to take him down a notch. She couldn't help it. She hated the fact that he always knew everything. And now he was telling her to get over it so they could be a team, because she was the one who always started it.

How embarrassingly immature of her--but only because he was totally calling her on it.

"We complement each other," he continued. "You are incredibly organized and knowledgeable and I have always admired that."

Katie sank against the wall. He was complimenting her? This wasn't the first time he had, but it was the first time she'd actually listened and believed it to be true, not part of some overarching game. That was the difference. She'd been competing with him, but now he wanted a teammate.

However, you couldn't always trust men, though. Take Will, for example. She'd bought him a five hundred dollar car stereo system, thinking she had to balance out an engagement ring. Now it turned out she was going to be one of many gracing the gift returns line in the city after the holidays. Couldn't her ex at least hinted that he was leaning toward "I don't" instead of "I do"?

"Now that there is no longer a conflict of interest between us, can we work together in harmony, Katie?"

She struggled to comprehend Nash's words.

His coat brushed her Rudolph the Red-nosed Reindeer nursing scrubs. "Can we?"

"Um…" Her voice squeaked. "What conflict of interest?"

"I'm no longer stealing your best friend from your brother."

Katie had to look away. Elephant in the room recognized and confirmed? Checkity-check-check-check.

It was true, though. She--and the majority of Blueberry Springs--hadn't given him an easy time when he swept in and wooed Beth, while Katie's brother, Oz, tried to get his life together so he could return to his soul mate.

"Friends?" Nash's voice was low, hope evident in his sharp blue eyes. His wonderful shoulders were frozen, waiting for her to say yes and make things easy. Or crush him with a no.

How could she do that to a man like him?

Easy. She was Katie Reiter. He was Nash Leham.

However, she couldn't. Not today. Call it a flash of holiday goodwill, or intoxication by a scent that should be outlawed around women who were on the rebound, but she nodded. She shook his hand, ignoring the zing that tore through her at his touch.

"Fine," she said. "Friends. Nash. Dr. Leham." Crap. Which side was she on now? This was confusing. "What *do* you want me to call you?"

"Nash is fine." There was a hint of a rogue smile curving his lips, and Katie wondered if years ago he had, indeed, been intentionally, and with well-disguised gusto, volleying those shots back to her all those years ago. But most of all, if she was about to get slammed now that she'd temporarily let her guard down.

"I HEARD YOU WERE BACK, Nash Leham!" Liz crowed, cradling her left hand, which was well-bandaged. "How long this time?" She pushed Katie aside to give the doctor a half hug.

"You didn't have to injure yourself to come see me," Nash scolded, taking a seat near the gossip.

"Oh, you," Liz said, blushing as she tapped Nash's thigh with her good hand. Katie gaped in wonder. Liz? Blushing? Over Nash? Had to be the cologne. It had a wild and far-reaching effect.

Katie turned to him. "Weren't you in favor of scent-free hospitals?"

Nash glanced away almost sheepishly. "I forgot. So!" he said brightly to Liz, who was preening her gray-streaked hair. "Let me guess...cut yourself preparing a Christmas Eve feast?"

"No, wait," Katie interrupted. "That's not something you would forget, Nash--Dr. Leham. Uh, Nash." She turned to Liz for support. "Am I right or am I right?"

"She does have a point," the reporter agreed.

"I wanted to smell good," he muttered as he inspected Liz's bandage. "Now about your hand."

"Subsection 8.1.7." Katie grinned, gleeful to have that one memorized. "You might also care to know that the penalty is a day's pay." Oh, she had him now.

"Upon second warning."

Darn. Of course he had more memorized than she did.

The doctor returned his attention to the patient. "Brussels sprouts?"

"How did you know?"

"I've seen the way you cut them. This was bound to happen. Didn't I tell you that?"

Liz looked contrite. "You did."

Okay. This was weird. Not only had he changed, but he'd somehow dazzled Liz into liking him--a lot. And the professional shield he used to wear had been replaced by... warmth. Caring. He'd always cared, of course, but this...this was...Katie *liked* this.

But something was up. He wasn't a man who *forgot* and wore cologne to work.

"Katie, could you pass me fresh gauze? The two-inch." Nash had unwound Liz's bandage and was waiting for Katie's help. She flew into action, grabbing a stack of four-inch squares as well as antiseptic. She fumbled as she handed them to him.

"You okay?" he asked, setting down those supplies to reach for the ones he wanted.

"Right. Yes, of course." She felt like a nurse on her first day, and could tell he was enjoying throwing her off guard. But instead of wanting to punch him or declare it "game on," Katie eased her stool closer to him, curious to find out whatever else was different about him.

Was he still a big jerk?

Was he still single? What if he was married and had kids?

And why was disappointment igniting within her at the thought of him being happy with someone else?

They slowly fell into a quiet work rhythm where words weren't required, while Liz nattered away, asking all the questions Katie wanted answers to.

Kids? No.

Married? No.

Seeing someone? No.

Still heartbroken over Beth? No.

Were they still actually friends? Yes.

Was he looking to start a new relationship? Yes.

Did he want Liz to hook him up with her niece, Nicola, who'd just moved to town? No.

Did he make management level in the city? Yes. (Come on, Liz. Everyone knew that.)

Liking the city? Missing Blueberry Springs.

Katie laughed, breaking their wordless working spell. "You miss Blueberry Springs? Yeah, right."

Those icy blue eyes were on her again. "I did."

"Why?" She didn't mean to sound as if she was scoffing. But really, why would Mr. Fancy Management Pants want to come back *here*? What was there to miss for a person such as Nash, who was always looking for the next rung up the promotion ladder?

Those eyes. They kept staring at her. Poking. Delving. Finally, he said quietly, "I missed the people."

Right. That wasn't it. He was definitely up to something. She broke eye contact and began tidying up. "Keep your hand dry for at least forty-eight hours, Liz."

Nash interrupted, taking over the dos and don'ts of suture care, leaving Katie biting her bottom lip to keep from telling him off.

"You two sure work nicely as a team," Liz said when he finished his spiel. "Did you hear Katie and Will broke up? She's single, you know."

Nash gave Katie a glance out of the corner of his eye. "I heard, yes."

"Katie has very good style. I think the two of you would make a fine couple." Liz eyed her speculatively. "You're looking trim, Katie. Volleyball? Or are you dieting? You know who is dieting? Jen Kulak." She turned to Nash. "She's the new nature guide who almost burned down the town." Liz addressed Katie again. "I'm sure of it. She lost a lot of weight when she moved here a couple of years ago. But that's good. When she gets pregnant it will be much easier to tell." She laughed.

"Liz, did you need anything for the pain?" Katie began ushering her out of the room, her winter apparel bundled in her arms. "I heard there's a storm coming, so you should likely head home while you can."

"Not coming until tomorrow." Liz pushed against Katie, angling herself to call out to Nash, who was escaping. "Let me know if you change your mind about my niece. You are a fine catch and it would be a shame for you not to pass on those genes, if you know what I'm saying?"

True that, sister.

Wow. Okay, Katie needed to go stick her head in a snowdrift. She'd officially...well, she wasn't sure what, but it couldn't be good.

"Thank you, Liz. I'll keep that in mind," he said.

Katie forced herself to keep from whipping around to see if Nash was serious. Why would he be considering Liz's niece when, right in front of him, Katie herself had so much to offer-- including a lovely, volleyball-toned body?

Puhlease.

Oh, what was her problem? She was relieved to be single. The last thing she needed right now was a man complicating her life.

She sighed. A man *would* be nice, though. Except for the part where they dump you, unexpectedly, in a humiliating heap. And then there was tidying up after them. Reminding them to fold their laundry. Clean their apartment. Buy new clothes. Get off the couch and live a little.

And anyway, she was on the brink of change. At least that's what she kept telling herself. Any day, she was going to become an interior decorator. Any moment her life was going to change…

Right. And how was that going to happen if she never pulled up her lacy thong and got her butt cheeks in action in order to make it happen? That was why she was still working here as a nurse, feeling more worn-out than ever.

"How's your dad?" Nash asked, startling Katie out of her thoughts. Liz had paused to chat with someone down the hall, and cast them a curious glance.

"Oh, um, fine." Katie smiled and adjusted her scrubs. "Thanks."

"His heart has been good?"

"Yes. Thanks." That was the other thing holding her back: her father. Harvey Reiter had had a heart attack, literally, when Oz had told him he was quitting the Reiter and Son accounting business. Katie had scoffed at her brother for making a big deal about changing course and following his dreams. But now she kind of got it. It wasn't easy.

She smoothed her tresses, touching her candy cane hair band, which helped keep in place the wisps that had fallen out of her ponytail.

"Your mom is well?" Nash asked, walking with her to the nurses' station.

Katie crossed her arms. "Are you taking a course on how to be human? Why all the small talk?"

To her surprise, he laughed. "I'm glad you noticed."

She narrowed her eyes. "Maybe AA? You have to make amends to all those you've wronged in the past?"

The space between them seemed to have disappeared. She

could reach out, grab the stethoscope slung around his neck and pull him close. Really close. And then keep him there.

"Did I wrong you?" he asked quietly.

"No. Um, yes?" She was getting lost in his eyes. "Don't you have pencils to line up in a row on someone's desk or something?"

It was definitely too warm in here. The thermostat must be stuck. Either that or one of the continuing care patients had pilfered her keys to crank up the temperature in their nursing home as well as the rest of the ward again.

Liz sidled up to them and Katie, still unable to break eye contact with Nash, said, "Second thoughts on that Tylenol, Liz?"

"What are you two staring at?" the reporter asked.

Katie blinked, the spell broken. She leaped away from Nash, shooting him a dirty look.

"And here I thought you took all these holiday shifts to get away from your mother and her overexuberance with the festivities, Katie." Liz laughed. "Mary Alice will be delighted to hear she was right."

"About what?" Katie moved behind her station for protection.

Liz faced Nash. "Where are you staying?"

"What is Mary Alice right about?" Katie pressed. The woman, Liz's sister, held the title of the town's biggest gossip, which was not an easy feat, seeing as Liz worked for the newspaper. But if she thought she was onto something in regards to her, Katie wanted to hear it first.

"Oh, I'm just making conversation." Liz gave her a sweet smile that made her instantly suspicious. "Now where are you staying, Nash, dear?"

"The B and B."

"How do you like the their decorating style?" Katie asked. The place had kitsch and dried flowers, and 1990s floral patterns on everything.

"It is one of a kind," he replied with a small smile.

"My ride is here," Liz said. "Nash, good luck. If you have time, stop by for a rum and eggnog or a meal. Hear me?"

"Thanks, Liz."

"You bet, sugar plum." With a wink, she was off.

"Are you alone for the holidays?" Katie asked.

Nash's chin tipped up slightly as he studied her. "I already have an offer from Mary Alice, thank you."

"Wait. You think I'm inviting you to spend it with *me*?"

"You mean to say that you would send me to Mary Alice's, where you know I would be submitting myself to the gossip firing squad?"

"Um, yeah."

"Katie, why do you hurt me so? I thought we agreed to be friends."

There was a teasing twinkle in his eyes and Katie couldn't quite seem to glance away. He had eased closer to lean against the wall beside her, causing her heart rate to increase as his soft cologne wafted her way. He smelled *good*. He was perfect in so many ways that Will wasn't. And yeah, Nash wouldn't ever write her sappy love notes like Will had, but…

No, this was bad. She couldn't think about Nash. He was her best friend's ex. He was in the no-no, don't-touch zone.

He had likely smelled like this when he'd been here thirty-two months ago and it hadn't affected her then. Not one iota. There was absolutely no reason it should impact her now. Besides, it wasn't as though he was what she was looking for. He'd been divorced before he'd met Beth. In other words, two major relationships had failed. Men were commitmentphobes and Nash was angling to become their spokesperson, by the looks of things.

Although…you couldn't help who you fell in love with, and Beth hadn't really been his fault. Her heart had still belonged to Oz when they'd met.

Wait. Back up a second. Thirty-two months? How did Katie know that? And why was she trying to defend his ability to maintain a serious relationship? The man liked projects, and women on the rebound. That's why he'd fallen for Beth, and now he was here to...well, this was probably a good time to stop thinking.

Nash was watching her again. "I noticed your family has a few new holiday decorations on the lawn."

Katie sighed and sagged against the wall next to him. "You can't even see the lawn for all the kitsch. Scott--you remember him? Our only police officer? Well, he came by to ask Mom to not plug everything in at once or the town would lose power. It's out of control and has been since Dad's heart attack. I'm literally hiding out so she doesn't make my head explode."

Her mother, Angelica Reiter, put on a bigger and bigger shindig each Christmas, thinking this holiday season would be her husband's last--even though he had been doing fine since his health crisis. While Katie had been freaked out when her dad had his heart attack, her mom's frenzied celebrations got to her in a place she wished she could compartmentalize far, far away.

Nash tapped her hand. "You okay?"

Katie pushed herself off the wall and scoffed. "Yeah, sure. Of course. I mean, yeah." She straightened a few stacks of papers at the station and cleared her throat. "I know you have Mary Alice's offer, but if that doesn't work out, my mom would be happy to have you."

"What about you?"

"It's her house."

"We don't have to be friends. If it makes you uncomfortable."

"No, I mean..." Katie sighed. It was so hard being strong sometimes. All she wanted was for someone to listen, fold his arms around her and allow her steal some of his strength for a few moments. Was that too much to ask? "Nash, just come. Okay? I'll be the miserable woman in the corner and you getting picked on by Oz will make my night."

"Beth will be there?"

"Of course. They live a few doors down and Oz is still family, even though I tried to convince my parents to put him up for adoption."

"Is she doing okay?"

"Yeah, of course. Happy. Um, beautiful."

"Always was." He seemed wistful.

"I mean she's pregnant. Again."

He nodded.

"You probably heard that from Mary Alice already?"

"I heard it from Beth first."

"Well, if you are up for it, Mom is serving dinner at seven-thirty. No need to RSVP."

Katie found herself holding her breath until he replied.

"That would be nice. Thanks."

There *was* something different about Nash. He was softer. Still buff, but softer around the edges personality-wise. More gentle and not so uptight. The lines around his eyes suggested a kindness he hadn't shown Katie before. Beth, yes. Patients, of course. But never her. Somewhere along the line, he'd become a good guy who was on her side, and she kind of wanted to roll around in that feeling as though it were her own personal catnip.

Well, except for the fact that he was probably coming over tonight to moon over Beth rather than to help Katie suffer through her overzealous mother's version of Christmas Eve.

"The buffer against my crazy mother will be the best gift anyone can give me at this point."

"You know how to make a man feel special."

"Got another stitch-up in ER room one," Amy said, passing them as she gave Nash's elbow a warm squeeze. "Seems to be a day for that. You two got it?"

"Yes," Katie said, making the turn to head back to the ER, Nash hot on her heels.

"Didn't Amy quit to go work at Brew Babies?" Nash asked.

"She did. She dated one of the bartenders, Moe, then decided when they broke up to become a nurse anesthetist. So she's back. She still takes regular nursing shifts, too, of course."

Katie entered the ER room to see the eldest sibling of the rash and reckless Mattson pack. "Devon Mattson, why am I not surprised?"

"Run-in with a Christmas tree." He didn't seem the least bit chagrined as he sat in his hospital gown, a handful of bloody gauze held against one of his marathon-strong thighs. The man was sexy in a lean sort of way, but he was too much of a daredevil. He was in need of a good woman to tame him. Or at least help him prevent stitch-ups every few months.

"You need to channel your inner calm and collected, Devon. As sweet as you are, who on earth would give you life insurance?"

He sent her a wicked grin. "You know you want to date me, Katie. That unexpected, fly-by-the-seat-of-your-pants side wants out to play."

Did someone growl? She wasn't sure if it was she or Nash. The doctor, however, seemed to be distractedly digging through supplies. Which was her job.

"I'm looking for a man who doesn't regularly require stitches. Thanks just the same." Katie began prepping a fresh suture kit for Nash, after elbowing him out of the way. "How did a tree do this, anyway?"

"Frankie and I were trying to surprise your mom with an aluminum one. We made it in his shop while I was trying to convince him to give my sister a ring for Christmas. Lights up and everything. I told Frankie I had it. I didn't have it."

Katie raised her eyebrows and handed Nash swabs as he began inspecting Devon's torn skin.

"Ow!" Their patient pulled his leg away. "Not so hard, buddy."

Nash muttered an apology. "Bit risky, placing a tree on top of a house in this weather, don't you think?"

"Yeah, sure." Devon was watching him warily. Suddenly, understanding lit up his blue eyes and he glanced at Katie.

"You're looking for someone steady and not into crazy risks. Right, Katie?"

"Of course. Why would I want a man who comes to the ER for stitches and not to drop off flowers for me?"

Devon laughed. "I sometimes can't believe you and my sister are friends. Maybe you can rub off on her." He laughed again. "Mandy's been consistently whooping my butt out on the race track lately and I need something to take her out of the game. Running her own restaurant hasn't helped so marriage and kids seems like the next logical plan. And she's already got Frankie. Just add a wedding."

Devon leaned back on the stretcher, propping himself up with his arms as he addressed Nash. "Katie needs someone reliable. Someone with a good job. Nicely dressed." He winked at her as if to say *I've got this one.* "Her last boyfriend wasn't much of a risk taker. But he was probably a bit too calm and collected--you know what I'm saying, Dr. Leham? Ow! Stop with the freezing already. It hurts worse than the stitches."

Another muttered apology came from Nash.

Katie exchanged the empty freezing needle for a prepped suture one.

"Anyway, her ex was too content to sit around and play video games. She needs a man who isn't going to throw curve balls of death, danger, and destruction, but at least gets out of the house. You like to get out of the house, right, doc? You know what I'm saying?"

Behind Nash, Katie narrowed her eyes and shook her head in warning. Devon carried on. "You travel. Try new things. Help others. Didn't you do Doctors Without Borders? That's really cool, by the way. Adventure in a not-too-risky way. Can you take nurses with you for that?"

"Devon, do I need to call in Amy to put you under for this procedure?" Katie asked.

Nash let out an amused chortle, his hands shaking with held-in mirth.

"Don't you go stitching until you're done laughing, okay, doc?" Devon gave Katie an exasperated look.

Yes, someone like Nash would be perfect for her, but Katie would prefer the version that came without the jerk sauce she so despised.

"Wow, that was pretty fast," Devon said as Nash finished patching up his leg.

"We're a good team," he said. Katie met his eyes, which were full of admiration as well as satisfaction. She gave him a small smile and nod.

"How many stitches?"

"Twenty-five," Nash replied.

"Too bad Mandy says you hate each other, huh?" Devon said, testing his leg. "Otherwise you'd be a perfect match."

2

Katie ditched her scrubs and went downstairs to join Nash, who had come over with her after work. As she clacked down the steps in her heels, Nash reached out to help her with the last few.

"Is it warm in here?" she asked, briskly moving to the thermostat at the bottom of the stairs. Nope. Right on target.

"I think half the town is here," he whispered.

"Told you it was nuts. If I hadn't been working today I would have been here cooking at 5:00 a.m."

"The kitchen smells amazing. Rosemary and oregano with a bit of brown sugar."

"Be careful, my mom will think you're trying to scope out her secret recipe."

"The one for her stuffing? I already got it." He grinned as he flashed a recipe card covered in her mother's tight handwriting.

"She hasn't even shared it with me!" Katie made a grab for the card, just about knocking over an inflatable Santa propped near the staircase, but Nash, with a quick smile, flicked it out of reach.

"I have spent years winning over this town with my discretion and--"

"And inability to let it slip who took a pregnancy test or is knocking on death's door."

"Katie!" called her mother from the kitchen. The carol "Little Drummer Boy" began on the stereo and Oz's voice drifted out of the living room.

Katie slipped behind Nash, hoping to remain invisible for a few more moments. She'd already spent her weekend baking enough cookies to feed the entire town, or at least the massive crowd bursting out of her parents' living room. In fact, clusters of guests were drifting to the small corner where she and Nash were hiding, signaling that it was almost time to play mini hostess for her mother.

"That used to bother me quite a bit," Nash was saying, in regards to the fact that most of Blueberry Springs's medical staff didn't keep patient health matters particularly confidential. "In fact, while I know you and I never saw eye to eye on some things, I always appreciated your professionalism and quiet candor."

"Thank you." Katie placed a hand on his chest, aiming to redirect him so they could avoid Mary Alice. Electricity shot up her arm and Nash rested his hand over hers, his eyes bright. Everything in her body told her it had been too long since a man had gazed at her like that.

Wow.

"*Now* I know why you came back, you sly dog." Mary Alice's eyes crinkled with delight as she elbowed her way between the two of them.

"Because I missed you, of course," Nash answered, placing a chaste kiss on the older woman's cheek. "Lovely to see you, even though you haven't listened to your doctor's orders and quit smoking."

Mary Alice gave him a bashful smile that caused Katie's jaw to drop in shock. "I only smoke when I am stressed and missing my little Nashikins." She patted his cheek affectionately.

"All the time, then?" he replied.

"Not coming to my house for dinner? How about tomorrow?"

What in the name of all things holy had transpired between these two? Katie wondered. Mary Alice had practically run him out of town years ago and now the two of them were kind of gross, even if it was merely a platonic weirdness going on between them. "Mary Alice?"

The gossip blinked as though coming to, and took a giant step back, landing against Angelica Reiter and her tray of bacon-wrapped delicacies. They scattered across the floor, leaving snail-like grease trails.

Katie's mother gazed at Mary Alice in disbelief, then the two women dived for the appetizers, muttering about a thirty-second rule.

Nash and Katie shared a glance.

"Want a rum and eggnog?" she asked.

"I've heard about your mom's potent eggnog, so yes," he said quietly. "I think that would be in order."

Katie pushed him to the left, skirting the room that contained Beth and Oz. Ignoring her mother's hints about someone getting a cloth to wipe the floor, she ducked into the kitchen. If she started helping now, she wouldn't finish for days.

"There's my girl! The best nurse in town!" her father said, bursting in through the back door. "And hanging out with Dr. Leham."

Harvey gave her a wink, and she rolled her eyes. "He was spending the evening alone, Dad."

"Not what I heard, but lovely to have you choose our home tonight, Dr. Leham."

"Nash, please," the doctor insisted, shaking the man's hand.

Harvey leaned in to give Katie a kiss on the cheek. "Don't you look lovely. And I noticed your festive scrubs earlier. Good call, Angelica, dear!" he said loudly. He held a palm against his gut and winced. "Stay away from the cabbage rolls."

"They're fine. You're just eating too much," Angelica said from the doorway. Her curled bangs had stuck to her forehead and her necklace was off-kilter, but she was smiling.

"I need an extension cord," her husband said.

"What for?"

"Frankie, Devon, and I are placing Benny's star up on the roof."

"There's one in the car."

Her father stomped back out into the cold and Nash muttered, "The night shift might be looking at more sutures for the boys."

Katie smiled and adjusted her mom's pendant, then stepped back, bumping into the open fridge door. Beth Reiter, her sister-in-law and best friend, appeared as the door closed. She was also the ex-fiancée of the man who had gently rested a hand on Katie's waist so she wouldn't back into him. A warm hand that fell from her waist, leaving her feeling cold.

"Beth, you look lovely." Nash was around Katie in a flash, his lips on Beth's cheek, which was turned up in offering.

"She glows," Katie said, clearing her throat, still unable to believe just how beautiful Beth was, four and a half months pregnant with her and Oz's second child. Her skin looked healthier than any commercial Katie had ever seen, and her hair had a glossy sheen that no amount of product or expert hands had ever been able to produce on Katie's own locks. "She should be on the cover of a pregnancy magazine."

Beth blushed and waved the compliment away. Oz came up behind his wife, nuzzled her neck and clenched her in a careful bear hug before looking up at Nash. "Hey."

"Seriously, Oz. Where are your manners?" Katie scolded. "Don't be so primal. You already pissed on her, dragged her back to your cave and forced her to carry your offspring. Twice. Try saying hello nicely."

"There wasn't much resistance," Oz said, his eyes on Nash.

"All right. Who wants eggnog?" Katie began sloshing the drink into cups, handing them out and hoping her mother hadn't skimped on the rum--which she had done the year after Oz ended up in the drunk tank due to indulging in a bit too much in hopes of soothing his broken heart, courtesy of the two ex-lovers standing mere feet apart.

Thank goodness Will had just up and left Katie. It made for a clean break. A fresh start. Sort of inspiring and exciting, if she thought about it, actually.

Hmm. Shouldn't she feel more heartbroken?

Nah, probably not. Anyway, it was hard to mourn when you still had hope. Hope that your man would come back for you. Then Will and Nash could fight over her, Neanderthal-style, as Nash had over Beth. Total turn-on.

Katie almost laughed. Nash would fight with her, yes. Over her, no. Her mind was running away without its good friend, logic.

"You okay?" Beth asked, pulling her aside.

"Of course. What makes you think I'm not?"

"You gave me spiked eggnog."

"Really, Beth. A little alcohol won't hurt..." Katie scrunched her eyes, fighting off the desperate feeling that was washing over her. Envy. She wanted what her best friend had.

She switched Beth's cup for one from the unspiked bowl, then herded her friend, her sibling, and Nash into the dining room, where her mother had begun ordering people to serve themselves.

A massive turkey dinner with all the trimmings was laid out, along with egg rolls, cabbage rolls and so many other dishes Katie didn't know where to start. She picked up a pile of wreath-patterned paper plates and began passing them out, to help keep the buffet line moving.

"I'm surprised you didn't buy more of these holiday-themed fold-up chairs," she joked to her mother as she whisked one forward for Beth's grandmother. The chair backs were printed with Elvis Presleys dressed as Santa.

"That was all they had." Her mother wrung her hands and frowned, the line between her eyes deepening as she calculated the number of chairs and people needing them. Katie felt a pang of compassion for the woman. She understood wanting everything to be perfect, and if this had been her own shindig, she'd be two sheets to the wind by now in order to try and combat the stress of it all.

"It's fine, Mom. You've done well. People can sit on the stairs and floor. They won't mind."

"I need to check on the pies." Her mother hurried off and Katie turned to find Nash and Oz glowering at each other from across the room.

The front door banged shut and Katie stepped around the corner to greet her father. "You look pale," she said, taking his coat. "You feeling all right?"

"Just about fell off that roof, is all."

"Dad!"

"What? It's nothing. I'm here, aren't I? And the star is in place. Where's the food?"

Katie pointed to the mob surrounding the table. Her mother had checked on her pies and was now scolding her nephew, Justin, about how he'd made Katie work the holiday. Katie gave her cousin a small shake of the head, letting him know she'd knee him in the chestnuts roasting over his personal fire if he so much as let on that she had more to do with her taking those shifts than he did.

To her left, she overheard someone asking Nash why he didn't fight harder for a nice woman like Beth, when he had all those fancy things to offer. A pang of guilt hit Katie and she moved through the crowd to edge him somewhere safe.

Justin's smile tightened as Katie gave him an extra glower for good measure before reaching Nash. Her cousin turned away slightly, code for "Message received. Like my nuts. Will not rat you out."

She owed him one. And she owed Nash, too. But how would she ever repay him? She still barely even liked him.

"I AM SO SORRY, NASH." Katie settled herself next to the doctor near the backyard fire pit. She'd managed to carve out the drift the small bench was hiding in, and set them up with a cozy little blanket-lined niche to enjoy their meal away from all the hubbub and nosy questions. Gentle flakes drifted down to rest on their coats, melting slowly in the fire's heat.

"Sorry for what?" he asked.

"For that." Katie waved a hand toward the house, where the windows were fogged, lights and merriment giving it a contented glow.

"I knew what I'd be facing by coming back."

"Then why did you do it?"

"I was starting to feel as though I'd left something important behind." He used a stick to poke at the fire. "Like I had overlooked something good. I figured the best way to sort it all out was to come visit." He tossed the stick in the flames. "And what better excuse than filling in for Dr. Nesbit?"

Katie swallowed. Why did it feel as though he was talking about leaving *her* behind? Had being on the rebound finally kicked in with its steel-toed boots, causing her to lust after the first man who came along? Because why would Nash come back for her, of all people? She'd never once given him an inkling of hope that they could be anything more than fire and water.

"Plus," he continued, "I owed Dr. Nesbit a favor for helping me once. The least I could do was help him out during the giving season. Because despite what you might think, I'm not all evil, Katie."

The crackling of a log broke the silence.

"I wouldn't be sitting here if I thought you were evil," Katie said quietly.

"Thanks. And for making sure I wasn't alone tonight. Or being pumped by Mary Alice." He smiled.

"But what about tomorrow? It's Christmas. Where will you be?"

"I'm working."

"So am I. Our shifts don't last all day, unfortunately."

"I'm not inviting myself to family events."

"You're at this one."

"Hardly family." Setting his plate aside, he gestured to the stuffed house.

"Blueberry Springs is family, and you used to live here, so you don't get a free pass into spending Christmas alone."

He gave her a soft smile and she felt herself getting too comfortable.

"You and your stupid budgets," Katie went on. "You know how much crap I got on my fingers when you decided we could save a thousand dollars a year on toilet paper in order to help fund that new MRI machine?" She held up a mittened hand. "Way too freaking much!"

He was close to her, his eyes a perfect blue. Mesmerizing. Intelligent.

She sniffed and turned away. Those eyes were part of the man who used to infuriate her, and she was in trouble right now because she couldn't find that fury. She couldn't even dig into that anger behind the long-ago TP injustice. All she could think about was how his MRI machine had saved her nephew.

Nash had edged closer. She didn't know whether to lean in or stand up.

"The MRI machine helped save little Benji when he fell off the change table at Benny's restaurant a few months ago," she finally said.

"Beth's son?"

"Yeah. My brother's little guy."

Nash kissed her. He leaned in, his lips against hers. And while she loved the warmth of his wet tongue against her cold lips, all she could think was that he wanted to be kissing her best friend, Beth, not her.

"Are you happy, Katie?" he asked, so close she got lost in the clouds of their warm breaths.

"Happy?" she squeaked.

He'd said her name. He knew who he was kissing.

Her.

And suddenly that felt important, and so did his question. When had anyone asked if she was happy?

How about never.

"What's happy?" She placed her mitts on either side of his mouth and drew him closer, kissing away the cold freshness on his lips.

"I used to wonder the same," he murmured.

And then he'd found Beth. Lost her. Was likely here to try and get her back.

Katie needed to distract him. She pulled him close, giving him her best kiss, hoping to steal his mind, his thoughts. Maybe even save her brother and his hard-won marriage.

When Nash pulled back from her kiss, his blue eyes were clear and dreamy. "Katie Reiter, I had no idea you could kiss like that." He cozied up to her again and for a second she wondered whether this really was about her and not Beth.

Was it Katie's turn? Her competitive edge sharpened like a blade.

"I think there are a lot of things about me you don't know, Dr. Leham."

"Dr. Leham. Now you're calling me that." He shook his head in amusement.

Again that softer, teasing side she hadn't expected. Had he

really changed? Or was this the side that Beth had always seen and ultimately loved? The same side that had lured her friend into becoming his project--a project to turn Beth, a country gal who wanted nothing more than a family and comfy pair of jeans, into a sophisticated career woman?

"I think calling me something a little less formal might be more fitting." He tucked a strand of hair behind Katie's ear.

"What game are we playing?"

"Is this a game?" He drew her chin up so he could match his lips to hers.

Katie gently pushed him away. "I don't know. I'm on the rebound and you're..."

"What?"

"You're you." Divorced. Jilted groom. Former know-it-all jerk, possibly; the jury was still out on whether this new persona was for real or not. Best friend's ex... Those were just a few things that popped to mind.

"What does that mean?"

She faced the fire, arms crossed.

"Katie?" He slipped his gloved hand into her mittened one.

"You like things a certain way. Your way."

"So do you."

"And you are my best friend's ex."

He withdrew his hand. "Right."

They sat in silence, the warmth of the fire battling the air's chill.

"What happened with you and Will?"

Katie didn't answer.

"Did he finally drive you around the bend?"

It was a serious question, not meant to offend, but it hit a mark within her. "Excuse me?"

Nash draped an arm around her, keeping her close. "You are neat, organized, know what you want and won't let anything stand in your way. Will is a lot like your father--good with numbers, but content to sit back and let you lead. No matter how strong we are, sometimes we all need someone else to pull the wagon for a while." Nash paused as though collecting his thoughts. "Katie, you need someone by your side who can help kick the hurdles out of your way. Not doing it for you. Not watching you do it. You need a wingman." He turned her face to him again, eyes meeting hers. "You need me. Wouldn't you agree?"

Nash was really laying down the cards. He was cocky. Confident. Sure of himself and so incredibly correct in terms of what she needed in a man. And they *would* be an amazing team. They'd get stuff done. He'd understand where she was coming from.

But while he made a good argument, was he really the missing piece?

She stood. "I'm not sure we can do this."

"Is it the long-distance thing?"

"Best friend thing."

"Becoming best friends takes time."

"I meant Beth," Katie snapped.

"I can talk to her."

"No, I can."

"She and I are still friends," he said.

"Yeah, and so are we."

"Are we going to fight over who knows Beth best?"

"This is my hurdle, Nash."

"Then it is all yours."

Katie sat, fighting a smile. This? Yeah, okay, this could work. "Fine. But what are we actually doing? What are we asking her?"

She watched Nash's expression as he contemplated his answer, loving that she could talk so openly and bluntly with a man.

But this one? Oh, heavens. What was she thinking? This wouldn't last one second. And they were moving so fast it was ridiculous. This was what had happened with Beth. He'd come in, told her what she needed to hear and swept her away just like that.

Well, Katie was smarter than that.

"Maybe we need to slow down a little," Nash said quietly, drawing her against him as she sagged in relief.

They sat in comforting silence, and even though she knew that her family, best friend, and half the town were on the other side of the snowbank protecting them from gossip, it was nice to be held. To be with someone who seemed to be in sync with her.

Nash tossed another log on the fire and sat back, allowing her to snuggle against him again. "What do you want in life, Katie? Are you happy doing this?"

There it was again. Happy.

"Doing what?" she asked, buying time.

"Nursing. Being the bottom of the totem pole."

"I'm head nurse. A source of pride and gloating for my father, seeing as I failed bio the first time around, in tenth grade." She swung a fist through the air. "I sure showed them, by golly."

"There's more to you, Katie."

"Only when I eat a lot."

Nash shifted, taking a no-nonsense tone. "You and I are a lot alike, and I'm always wanting more. So? What are you looking for, Katie Reiter? Don't hide behind humor and topic changes."

She reached for her cup of rum and eggnog, teetering on the brink of telling him everything she'd kept inside for years.

No wonder Beth had crushed on him so badly; the man was a good listener. That was also likely why some folks had thought he might be gay. Style and listening skills? Not something you could drive by and grab off Main Street in the small mountain meadow town of Blueberry Springs.

"I want to get into decorating." Oh, crapola. Did that just come out of her mouth? She glanced in her empty cup. Dang rum and eggnog. The stuff was like a lethal injection of truth serum.

"Interior or cake?"

"I love that you asked that." This was not good. She was going to warm until she thawed, get all gooey and mushy for a man who...who what? She sighed. "Interior."

She had to stop talking to him. Couldn't someone have a heart attack or something? But not her father, of course. He'd already had his.

And that was yet another reason Katie needed to ignore the idea of getting into interior decorating. Her father would have a coronary if she dropped nursing, and she'd feel guilty until the end of time. She'd seen what going through a career switch had done to her brother, and it hadn't been pretty.

"I took a few online courses," she said. Holy moly truth serum. Had Nash slipped her a sodium pentothal? Why was she telling him things she hadn't even told Will in a moment of postcoital glow?

"Did you enjoy them?"

"Yeah, of course." Feeling uncomfortable, she got up and threw another log on the fire.

"Any experience?"

She shrugged. "A few friends here and there. Just as a favor. Nobody knows I have training or have been thinking about this."

The back door opened and Katie felt the surge of heat that came with getting caught doing something wrong. Secrets. So many secrets. She was glad she was no longer wrapped in Nash's arms, at least.

"Hey, you two." Mary Alice paused outside the door to fish a lighter from her coat pocket. "Hiding out together, are you?"

"Hardly. The house is packed." Katie blinked and poked at the fire. She *had* been hiding out. And with Nash, no less. Kissing. Snuggling. Sharing secrets and dreams. Allowing it all. Even enjoying it.

She'd never believed Beth had good taste in men--first falling for Katie's screw-up brother, and then Nash. But there were some good sides to Oz, who was proving to be an amazing father as well as a caring and doting husband. Nash, however? Katie had never seen the value in him other than the fact that he never seemed to need someone to remove the stains from his clothes as Will always had.

But now she kind of got it.

Mental note to herself: Nash was still Beth's ex.

The flame from Mary Alice's lighter flickered in the light breeze and Nash moved to help shield it.

"How was supper, Mary Alice?" Katie asked. "Did you get enough?"

"Sure did. Your father ate so much he's got a stomach ache. Your mother says it is not the cabbage rolls, so don't walk into that one." Mary Alice squinted as she took a satisfying drag on her cigarette. She smiled at Nash. "Thanks, hon."

He gave a nod and moved back to the warmth of the fire.

"So, Nash, how is being a bigwig in the city treating you these days?"

"It is what I was looking for," he replied carefully. Katie wanted to ask if it was what he was still looking for. She had a feeling it wasn't.

"If so, then what are you doing in this place?" Mary Alice laughed, her smoker's cough moving phlegm in a way that had to have Nash cringing and double-thinking his gentlemanly move to help her light her cancer stick.

"How's the store?" he asked diplomatically. "Still have that husband of yours kicking around?"

"You thinking of replacing him?"

"You're more woman than I could handle, Mary Alice."

"That's true," she said thoughtfully. "What about our fine Katie here? I've often wondered why the two of you didn't hit it off."

Katie rolled her eyes. "Have you not met Nash?"

"I have." Mary Alice crossed her arms and stared her down.

She took a final drag of her smoke, then chucked it in the fire, ignoring the mistletoe ashtray Katie's mother had set out on the snowy porch railing. "So you two? I was talking to Liz today."

"How's her hand?" Katie asked, heading her off.

"Fine enough. I heard you two are working together again tomorrow?"

"Yes," Nash replied.

"Well, I'll try to keep everyone out of the hospital for you." With a wink, Mary Alice stepped back indoors, leaving Katie to wonder what the woman saw when she looked at the two of them and if that something had actual potential.

3

*L*ast night Katie had made it through her mother's Christmas Eve party with no major incidents. She'd even managed to spend time with Beth and Oz without feeling too terribly guilty for a) reasons of kissing the ex, b) enjoying it, as well as c) spending time with him during dinner--although she could argue that Beth and Oz were married and had each other, whereas she had nobody and nothing but her (not quite) bitter, broken heart for company--and finally, d) for ignoring Nash a teensy bit in order to spend time with other people.

The problem was, neglecting Nash had opened him up for every single, eligible woman in Blueberry Springs to move in on him, which Katie had found surprisingly distracting. But really, it was good, because maybe all that flirty-flirt business would throw Mary Alice off the track.

Not that there was a track. Nash was her best friend's ex. That was a line you didn't cross.

For any reason.

Probably.

"Nurse Reiter."

Katie inhaled, bracing herself against that brisk voice she

35

hated so dearly. She turned, jaw set. "Yes, *Nash*."

Just like old times.

Except he grinned as though it was their own secret game, and she couldn't help but smile back.

Just like new times.

"Are you needing to cut nursing supplies for another major project of yours?" she asked with fake sweetness.

"I was thinking, since you are so good with PICC lines, you could use cheaper needles in order to leave the better ones for the other nurses. We'd save approximately twenty-three dollars over the course of the year. Be a sport and help out the hospital?"

She gave his chest a playful shove. "Merry Christmas Nash-hole."

He grabbed her arm, wincing in fake pain at the nickname. "Ouch."

She smiled and tugged her hand free so she could give him one of the emergency gifts she kept wrapped and under her basement suite's tree in case someone gave her an unexpected present. This morning it had felt right to print Nash's name on the tag. And not just as a bribe to keep him from spilling the beans about her wanting to go into decorating--not that she thought he would.

"For me?" he asked, clearly surprised.

"To take away the sting of my bites."

He let out a rich laugh and set his coffee down on the nurses' station.

"Hey! You can't eat and snack here. It is a rule we adhere to from years ago. An esteemed doctor--Nash Leham, have you heard of him?--put this rule into place and it is as highly regarded as he is."

"Katie, shut up. You had me at 'Hey' and that scary tone of yours. I won't snack or drink here." He sat in her chair, kicked his feet up on the desk and chugged his coffee, then set the mug down on her notes.

She spun the chair around so he faced her. Standing over him, she demanded, "What has gotten into you?" He set the wrapped box aside and stared at her, not answering. "Really! What?"

He glanced away and gave a small shrug.

She yanked the chair closer. She needed to know why he was in Blueberry Springs and why he was joking around and acting like a nice guy--a guy she could totally fall for. She gave the chair a rattle. "What?"

"I got lonely, okay? I was fine chasing my career before I came out here, but now…I just… It got under my skin, okay?"

The shock of his confession knocked her sideways. "Do you want to move back?"

"I don't have the energy to go through all that renovation and decorating stuff in Blueberry Springs again."

"I could do it." She waited, not daring to breathe or blink.

"I couldn't ask you to do that."

"You'd pay me, so yes, you could. I hated your old place, because it wasn't Beth's home and it represented everything you were trying to change in her. However, stylistically, it was gorgeous. I think you still need something sleek, fresh, and with strong lines. Practical, efficient storage to keep you organized, but with a modern, yet classic style. Simple lighting with an open concept would suit you."

"Bullcrap baffles brains. That's just a lot of jargon."

She narrowed her eyes. "Challenge accepted, Nash Leham."

He rocked back in her chair, smiling.

"You know how your old place had that island between the kitchen and the sitting area?" she asked. When he nodded, she continued, "It was too wide and too high. It stopped conversation and I'll bet that bothered you. You liked how it closed off the kitchen, but when you entertained, it felt like a barrier."

He paused thoughtfully. "How did you know that?"

"I'm that good."

A slip of a smile was her reward and she pushed the chair

away in triumph. It was either that or kiss him, and a woman had to remember where to draw the line.

"Hey," said a soft, slightly confused voice.

Katie turned to find Beth watching them. Katie pointed at Nash and cleared her throat. "He's still a stubborn jerk who wants things his way and doesn't think others measure up to his level." She dusted her hands together, ignoring Nash's hurt look. "You made the right choice, Beth."

"Baby, I've changed," he said in a flat voice, hands out to Beth. He wasn't even trying.

Watching Nash react to her words, Katie learned three important truths. He hadn't come for his ex. He hadn't been playing a game. He was back. Back for Katie.

It was time to stop thinking again.

"I brought this for you." Beth placed a warm drink on the counter. She adjusted her pink woolly hat over her chestnut curls. "I left you one in the ER, Nash."

"Thanks." He gave her a friendly peck on the cheek, snagging Katie's gift as he went. "Merry Christmas."

The women watched him move down the hall, and Katie hoped Beth wouldn't ask too many questions.

Beth took Katie's seat, rubbing her swollen stomach through her coat. "So? What's up between you and Nash?"

"He's still a pain in my backside."

"Huh. I thought he seemed different."

"Well, yeah, kind of," Katie said. She *had* kissed him without imploding. That implied change, didn't it?

"If you're being mad at him for my sake, I'm past it. And I think he is, too." Beth focused on the distance. "It seems important to him to patch things up between the two of you. He sounded worried about you when I told him about Will."

"You talked to him about my breakup?"

"Sure." She gave a small shrug. Then her eyes flashed with inspiration. "You two should date."

"No." Katie backed away. "I don't think that would be a good idea." It would be a *fabulous* idea.

"Why not? You guys would be perfect. All neat and anal about your ideas. And he's really a great guy. He just wasn't the one for me."

"But good enough for me?"

"Oh, silly you. It's probably just my pregnant brain talking and wanting everyone to pair up. He was really committed, plus he's the kind of man you need, because he won't put up with your bull."

"Okay, I've heard enough. Book the chapel on your way home."

"I'm serious." Beth rocked to her feet, her hands out for balance.

"Be careful on your drive," Katie said, catching her friend and directing her toward the hall that led to the parking lot. "A bad storm is coming through. You'd better head home." And never talk to Nash about this idea, because at the rate things were going, he didn't need support. She did.

***

KATIE STOOD inside the ER doors, mesmerized at how fast and hard the snowflakes were falling. There was already a foot on the sidewalks. With a grin, she smoothed her ponytail. If this snow kept up, she'd be stuck at work overnight. Not something most people wished for on Christmas Day, when there was a delicious turkey waiting for them after work. But then again, most people didn't have a mother who had gone nutso for the holidays and had terrified them with so many decorations their head spun like a pinwheel just thinking about it.

Her mom had called at 5:00 a.m. to ensure Katie could find her Christmas cardigan--which she was to wear over her Christmas-themed scrubs, which were to go over her holly turtleneck, which was, of course, over her--yes, her mother went that far--mistletoe lingerie. Not to mention the Santa socks, the light-up Christmas tree earrings, the jingle bell hair elastic, and Rudolph pin complete with a blinking nose.

Katie was ready to jump in a snowbank and hope for an avalanche rather than face her mother and yet more holiday cheer. Or admit to anyone that she had, in fact, dressed herself this morning.

What would her mom do tomorrow when Christmas was officially over? Would she go into a deep depression as withdrawal set in? Or would she start planning how she could make next year even bigger and better? Possibly, Katie might slip her a sleeping pill, as the woman had to be exhausted by now.

Turning away from the falling snow that was morphing the parked cars in the lot into hibernating bear humps, Katie moseyed down the quiet halls to the nursing station. Most patients who could be released had gone home to spend the holidays with their families. The rest would likely be having company later on tonight, assuming the roads were still passable.

Humming "Jingle Bells," Katie rounded a corner and bumped into Nash. She flicked his tie, which sported snowflakes. "All these flakes look suspiciously alike."

He smiled and smoothed his tie back into place under his doctor's coat before she could adjust it for him. "How's the weather looking?"

"I think we may end up stuck here for the night. The wind is expected to kick up as well."

Nash leaned against the wall to study her. "You truly are *happy* to be stuck here?"

"I am."

"Is it because I'll be here?" he teased. "Or are you trying to get out of your Christmas dinner invitation?"

Katie tried to ignore the blush that stole across her cheeks, burning a trail. "Or maybe because I get to avoid an even larger production than you witnessed at Chez Reiter last night."

"French?"

"I do believe my accent is better than yours."

"That was not how you say Louboutin," he said with a thick French accent, resurrecting an old battle.

She moved closer. "I do believe it is."

"And have you ever been to France?"

"Have you ever taken me?" she retorted.

He leaned in, his lips almost touching hers. "Do you want me to?"

"You could take me anywhere."

Oh, man. What was she doing? She was practically begging Nash to take her to bed. In France. Definitely not in the day planner. Not that one.

But it should be. Someone hand her a pencil. No, make that a permanent marker.

"Really?" he asked, his voice low. He still wasn't touching her, kissing her. But desire flashed in his icy eyes.

He would be good in bed, she thought. *All that fire. It would translate into hot, sweaty sex for sure.*

Trey, a teen who worked in the hardware store and had picked up a few housekeeping shifts at the hospital over the holidays, tore by, his slushy boots squeaking, chunks of damp snow falling off his coat. He dangled a plastic piece of mistletoe over Nash and Katie, stretching to do so.

"Kiss! You're under the mistletoe."

They didn't need prompting. Nash's arms--surprisingly strong--tugged her tight against his body. Katie pressed her palms to his chest, unsure whether she should push him off with a laugh or perform a tonsil check with her tongue. There was a reason not to kiss him, even in a jolly, festive, platonic way, but darn if she could recall what that was.

Or what platonic meant.

His lips were demanding. *Demanding what, exactly?* she wondered. Reciprocity. He was challenging her.

Challenge accepted.

He was not coming out on top. She would be the one leaving *him* panting, thank you very much. She kissed back, hard, putting everything she had into outdoing him. She pulled her sexiest moves, and his body responded against hers.

"Okay, that's enough!" Trey snapped. "My arm is getting tired. Besides, I thought you two were, like, rivals or something?"

"Still are," Katie murmured as she broke the lip-lock. Her eyes felt heavy with seduction and she didn't want to remove her hands from Nash's chest. He felt good. Right.

How could *that* be?

"Completely hate each other," Nash replied, his arms still tight around her.

"Right, then. I'm off to give Lauretta a chance with Gran's boyfriend, Reggie. Ciao."

Nash loosened his grip at the mention of his ex-fiancée's grandmother, and Katie stepped back, breaking their embrace completely.

She felt cold standing in Trey's puddle of melted snow.

She couldn't seem to break eye contact with Nash. Their flirting had slipped under her skin, the kiss sealing the deal.

She was officially in lust with her best friend's ex.

All Katie had to do was take one step forward and she'd be back in Nash's arms. Only this time she didn't have an excuse. Granted, there was no excuse for the way she'd kissed him only seconds ago. Mistletoe or not.

"So we might get stranded here? Together?" Nash asked, his voice throaty and deep. He couldn't seem to pull his attention away from her lips.

"Baby, it's cold outside." She was easing closer. Leaning in, inhaling his scent, memorizing it for the forbidden fantasies she'd surely be enjoying later.

"Dr. Leham!" Amy scuttled around the corner, halting abruptly when she spotted Katie. "You're needed in the ER."

He'd been leaning in, too, Katie noticed as he straightened. So quick, he practically took the air with him.

"Katie, you'd better come, too." The nurse's voice was stern and serious.

Katie and Nash fell into step, hurrying down the hall. As Katie rounded the corner to the ER, she almost laughed, feeling as though she was filming a medical drama and the credits were about to roll, with the two of them racing to save the day. Her breath left her chest as she spotted the patient sitting on a gurney, clutching his midriff.

"Dad! Is it your heart?" She knew it wasn't; he was clutching the wrong part of his body. But seeing her father in pain pretty much negated her nursing degree.

"I don't think so," he gasped. He leaned on Katie's shoulder as she wrapped an arm around him. "I'm glad I have the best nurse in town to help me. No offense, Amy."

"None taken," the other nurse grumbled.

"Appendix? Gall bladder?" asked Angelica. She was hovering, her eyes so wide they amplified the whole reindeer thing she had going on with her antler headband and Rudolph sweater.

"Dad," Katie said carefully, "is this the same pain you were having last night?"

"It wasn't the cabbage rolls," Angelica informed the group. She placed a hand on her daughter's wrist. "Dear, I told you your Christmas outfit would come together. You look lovely. Such a ray of sunshine for your patients."

A ray of sunshine. Yes, she was. She blinded them with too much Christmas whenever she entered a room. Add eye exams to every patient on the floor, please.

"I'm sorry I'm ruining Christmas," Harvey said to his wife, as Nash had him lay back for an examination. "I know how much tonight means to you."

"Well, then, you'd better get fixed up so we can head home before that turkey dries out." Angelica seemed to be half teasing, half serious. She dabbed at her eyes and turned away.

"There is plenty of food even if it dries out," her husband said. "Ow!"

"Hurts more when I touch there?" Nash said gently, as he probed the man's abdomen.

"Yes." Harvey gasped again as he tried to curl away from the doctor's touch.

"Call Oz," Katie told her mom. "He can walk over and check on the turkey. This will take some time." She turned the thermometer's reading so Nash could see it. They shared a look.

"I have so much left to do." Her mother buried her head in her hands. "Oh, this Christmas is cursed. First you having to work, then Devon getting cut by his tree decoration, and now your father." She let out a plaintive cry, then straightened, her power-mom persona back in place. "Fix him up, Dr. Leham, Harvey has somewhere to be and work to do."

Her father let out a moan as Nash continued to tap and prod him. Katie knew from years of experience that her father's pain levels indicated something bad. Quite bad.

"Mom," she said firmly, "go call Oz."

"Go home, Angelica," Harvey said, sitting up. "Go home." A sheen of sweat broke over his forehead and he appeared ready to vomit. Katie passed a kidney-shaped emesis basin to Nash, who had it under her father's chin in the nick of time. Harvey coughed and wiped his mouth with the back of his hand. "The weather is worsening. Go. I'll be home right after you."

"And how will you get home, mister?" Angelica asked, placing her hands on her hips in a way that made Katie realize things were going to break loose if she didn't take control. Her mother was trembling, her worry and fear for her husband taking over her nervous system.

"Mom, go call. Let Dr. Leham finish his examination, okay?"

Angelica hovered near the door, biting her thumbnail. "The turkey will be fine for a few more minutes. I can wait."

"Go," Katie said, her voice low.

Her mother turned and left the room, the welcoming scent of cinnamon and cloves following her.

"You're calling me Dr. Leham again?" Nash whispered to her as he washed his hands in the sink. His shoulders were stiffer and higher than usual.

"Respectfully, yes," she said with an exasperated glance. "Nothing more."

"Don't cross her when she gives that look," her father warned, then groaned again in pain.

"Dad, Nash isn't…" Katie floundered for the right thing to say, since technically her dad hadn't said anything, even though it was all laid out in his tone. And his tone warned Nash as though he was Katie's man.

"Whatever you say, Katie doll," Harvey replied.

"Don't listen to him. The pain has gone to his head." Katie struggled to busy herself so she'd have an excuse to not meet Nash's bright, inquisitive, and oh-so-smart-and-delving eyes. She bent over the chart, double-checking the information the intake nurse had written down.

"Whatever you two decide to do with each other, that's fine by me," her father continued. "If I die, you have my luck Dr. Leham, as well as my blessing."

"Thanks, Dad, but that won't be necessary, we only work together." She put the chart on the gurney beside him and noticed his red corduroy slacks. "Hey, I thought we threw these pants out last year."

"Your mother found them."

"My word. We'll have to burn them so they can't come back to haunt you." They were baggy, worn at the knees, and generally a crime against fashion.

"Please do."

"I'm going to have to agree, although that garment isn't going to be the worst thing about your evening, Mr. Reiter," Nash said. He sat on a stool beside her father and Katie felt her eyes tear up unexpectedly. He was being so kind, gentle, thoughtful, and caring with her dad... Well, heck. The lust had just turned into something else. Something mushier. Something she'd only read about in romance novels. The ones she vehemently denied reading. And if she was going to go full confessional, it was also something in scenes she rewound over and over again in her chick flicks and soap operas. And here she was, all ready to swoon over a doctor as though she was an old-fashioned heroine.

She kind of liked the feeling.

"I think you have acute appendicitis and are in danger of rupture. We will be removing your appendix. Immediately." Nash paused between each sentence to allow her father to absorb the news.

"Let's do it. I'm needed home by five."

"Mr. Reiter, you will need to be under observation after surgery. I don't think you are going home tonight."

"Please?" Harvey reached out, placing a hand on Nash's. Katie watched the men, feeling as though she should disappear. To see her father in a weak moment was not what she'd come to work for. She came here to be strong, the one in charge, and she wanted to scream at her father to be stronger. "I need to be home. This night is very important to my wife," he was saying.

"I understand."

Katie couldn't help but give Nash a hopeful, pleading look as well. Even though she knew there was no way her dad was going home tonight.

"I'll see what I can do to ensure Angelica's party isn't spoiled, but I can't make any promises." Nash turned to Katie, ushering her toward the door. "Scrub up, you're assisting."

"But I don't operate!" Katie backed up and hit the wall behind her.

"You do today. I need Amy for anesthesiology."

"But she's just a nurse. There's no anethesiologist on today, and he's family. You need more staff."

"There's nobody else here and we don't have time to wait." Nash was doing that pause-between-sentences thing again. "If I'm bringing someone inexperienced into the operating room, I'm bringing in the brightest."

"That's my Katie doll," Harvey said, groaning as he curled into a ball of agony on the gurney.

———

KATIE'S HANDS trembled as she finished prepping her father for laparoscopic surgery. She'd already shaved and cleaned the area where Nash would make his small incisions, and as she worked she kept up a steady stream of banter to keep herself distracted.

Her father was a good man. She hoped she didn't do something that would cause his untimely…

No, don't think that way.

This was a standard operation, one Nash could do unassisted, if need be. But he wouldn't need to. She was here. She knew her stuff. Or at least enough. He would be able to tell her where to be and when. They were a good team, and as he'd said, she was bright. All you needed to do was be in a few operations--which she had in school--and you had a pretty good lay of the land.

Stay out of the way.

Stay clean.

Don't kill the patient.

So here she was, ready to slice open her father. Well, not Katie herself; her hallway kisser would be doing that. Not that he was hers. Not yet.

Maybe not ever.

She rubbed her face and Nash frowned.

Realizing what she'd done, Katie turned on her heel and left the operating room to scrub up again. That was a stupid, rookie move, touching her face. *Way to prove yourself, Katie.*

The door swung open and the doctor joined her in the sterile light, probing her with his intense gaze.

"You okay?"

"Yeah, fine." She finished scrubbing, snapped on new gloves and smiled falsely.

"Your father needs you at your best in there. This appendix could rupture and if it does--"

"Yeah, I know." Katie brushed past him and his delicious green scrubs, hands up so she'd remember not to touch anything this time. "Hey, Dad!" she said as she entered the operating room once again. "Ready?"

"Sure, sweet pea. I'm glad you're here." He reached out to hold her hand, and after hesitating briefly, Katie took his and squeezed. When your father needed you, what was another pair of gloves and a scrub-up anyway?

"I love you, Dad."

"What? Am I gonna die?" He was lying on his back, his eyes glazed from the painkillers. "Save that for after the operation. Your mother already sobbed all over me."

Katie laughed, blinking away tears that welled up. "Sorry to break your heart, but I think half her upset was over her party."

"I'm feeling better now. No more pain. Maybe I could go home?" he said hopefully, as Amy positioned herself at his head. She adjusted tubes, cords, and a million other things Katie didn't know the first thing about. She hoped Amy knew what she was doing and could do it on her own.

"You have to stay here," Katie replied. Nash stood to the side, waiting, giving them time. Amy nodded and Katie placed a hand on her father's forehead to comfort him. "Amy's going to put you under now, okay? You won't feel a thing."

The other nurse began counting down backward.

"It's not working," her father said.

"Five, four…"

"I'm still awa--" And he was out. Just like that. Midword.

Katie looked at Amy in awe. "Can you do that to my mother sometime?"

She grinned. "Favorite part of the job. I cut the rector's wife off in the middle of saying 'shitake mushroom.' Guess where she stopped talking."

"You didn't."

"Sure did. She was giving me a hard time for engaging in premarital sex. So, you know. I made her swear." Amy shrugged.

Nash positioned himself over the patient, his focus narrowing in on the operation he was about to perform.

"Sorry," Katie said to him, "I'll be back in a flash." She left the room and once again repeated her scrubbing up and glove changing routine.

He was waiting, scalpel in hand, when she returned. She fell into an easy rhythm across from him, her earlier emotions washed away by purpose. Save the patient.

The body beneath Nash's deft fingers was no longer her father. This was a job. A project. A puzzle to fix and sort. A wrong to right.

She didn't flinch as Nash's scalpel opened the skin. She clamped, dabbed, suctioned, passed tools, and when she could afford the slight distraction, watched in awe as Nash, concentration turning his expressive blue eyes intensely bright, worked steadily and with a confidence that turned her on. Totally inappropriate. To be scoping out a surgeon, getting a bit flirty on the inside, when her father's life was in the man's hands.

But you didn't get to choose who you fell in lust with, did you?

"I really think we should celebrate New Year's Eve more," Harvey said, his voice still groggy and hoarse from the anesthetic.

"Why is that?" Katie asked. The operation had been a success and they were in the recovery room, monitoring his vitals and ensuring all was well, and continued that way. Her fifty-eight-year-old father was stable, yet a tad loopy.

"You could dress in a diaper. Get one of those horns with the streamers, and drink champagne."

"I think it's been done."

"Let's join them!" He pulled himself up, his balance off.

"Careful." Katie gently encouraged him to reposition himself on his back. "You'll hurt yourself."

Her father's eyes widened. "Did Dr. Leham mistake me for a piece of paper? Did he put staples in me?" He dropped the back of his hand across his forehead with a dramatic flourish. "Why didn't you *stop* him?"

"You only have internal sutures, Dad. Nothing to worry about. They dissolve."

"But staples? How do you remove them? You can't reach

inside and unclip them like a bundle of papers. I'll be setting off the metal detectors in airports. Subject to strip searches. I'll never be able to leave the country. What if they rust?"

And there was the father she knew. Not listening, and worrying over mostly nothing. Okay, pretty much nothing at all.

"Dad, you don't have staples. And besides, you don't fly anywhere. Have you ever even been in a plane?"

"Once." His eyes closed.

"Are you okay?" Her attention flicked to the monitors. All normal.

"It was ages ago. Your mother and I…" His voice took on a dreamy tone.

"How's he doing?" Nash asked from the doorway.

"A bit, um…"

"Trippy?" he suggested with a smile.

"Yeah." She glanced at their patient. He was snoring. Okay, then. Still groggy as well. She made a tick on her chart.

"He was awake for a bit?"

"He was."

"Coherent?"

"I'd say mostly. Yes."

Nash's warm hand rested on her shoulder for a moment and Katie couldn't help but wish he'd let it linger. "You did well in there."

"Thanks." *Tell me more.*

"It couldn't have been easy, but you were solid. I knew you would be." Another shoulder squeeze. She felt like a puppy begging for more treats.

"Thanks for helping him," she replied.

"Of course."

"Still snowing out there?"

"Roads are closed. Amy was saying Benny overheard people in his restaurant saying they probably won't open for another twenty-four hours."

"So we're stranded."

He flashed her a brief smile. "No Christmas dinner for you."

"I have snowshoes."

"The visibility is nil." He stood straighter, his face stern.

Katie glanced at her father. She expected protectiveness from him, not Nash. But wow. It was flattering.

She stood taller in turn. "Maybe I have snow goggles."

His eyes narrowed. "You're teasing me."

"A little. I don't have snowshoes."

He was so close. His eyes were so blue. She wanted to kiss him, and could tell he wanted to kiss her, too. Their desire was surging in the space between them, building as they breathed each other in. If they touched, sparks would fly.

She wanted to lean in, taste him.

"And so that's how I ended up flying a plane," her father said matter-of-factly.

Katie drifted back to reality, then jumped away from Nash. She had practically been kissing him, ignoring her ailing father, and was likely sporting a starry-eyed, drooling expression.

Surely her dad had noticed?

Nope. He was staring at the blood-oxygen monitor, holding his breath to make the numbers change.

"Dad, stop that!"

"I want 100 percent, but it's too hard. I'm trying for zero." He muttered a curse. "You made me breathe, Katie doll."

"Breathing is good. You want high numbers. Zero would make Mom very angry."

"Is she here?" He perked up like a boy expecting Santa.

"She managed to get back home to check on her turkey--only she can do that, apparently. And it sounds as though she's snowed in now. A lot has come down."

Her father tossed the blanket off his legs, eyes lolling back in his head at the sudden effort. "I need to go shovel for her!"

"No." Katie gently pressed him back into bed. "You can't go anywhere."

"But…" He pouted, then glared at Nash, who was watching from the doorway. "You--" he pointed a finger "--said I could go home after I got this dang-blasted thing out!"

"I said maybe. The day is still young, Mr. Reiter." Nash flashed a smile and hightailed it from the room.

Katie wished she could, too. Maybe follow him, then trap him in a broom closet for a little post-op shakedown. Because honestly? What was up with getting snowed in at work on Christmas Day and having your father around like a chaperone, when you could be getting it on with the most eligible man in town?

"KATIE, could I speak to you for a moment?" Nash stood in the doorway to the continuing care area, where she was checking on the residents. The gleam in his eyes had her up and across the room before she remembered to act cool.

Way too late for that now.

"Yes?"

He pulled her into the hall, double-checking to make sure nobody was listening. Katie almost laughed. There were no secrets in Blueberry Springs. For example, everyone had known Beth was pregnant almost before the mom-to-be did. They had known Devon's sister Mandy loved her best friend Frankie and that it was just a matter of time before they hit the sack and created magic. And everyone knew Jen Kulak, the local guide, hadn't burned down the forest. Oh, and Amber--daughter of one of Benny's long-standing waitresses, Gloria--had a new boyfriend who was away a suspicious amount of time. Not that Amber, who was gaga for the guy, seemed to see anything odd in that.

"You know how you were talking outside your parents' place last night about--"

Katie leaped on him, finger pressed to his lips. "Shh!" She glanced up and down the hall, then dragged Nash off, seeking somewhere more private.

More private, more private...where was that? The place was dead, but there was nowhere exactly private. Staff room? Amy could walk in. Operating room? Trey was cleaning it. ER? Someone might come in needing medical help. There was nowhere. Nowhere inside. She hip-checked the ER's side door and pushed, using it like a plow. The snow had piled up so much that even with the entry's mini overhang the drifts were blocking the way.

"You don't think people will be suspicious of us out in a snowstorm?" Nash shouted, above the wind howling through the doorway.

Shards of ice and snow stung her cheeks. Wow! When had all this blown in? Not too long ago there had been beautiful, fat flakes blocking out the midday sun. Now it was a raging midafternoon blizzard.

Katie pushed Nash back indoors. Well, mostly she hurtled back to his side, seeing as he'd been too smart to come out in the first place. He brushed the snow from her shoulders and smoothed her hair. "Cold enough for you?"

"Shut up," she muttered. "This is as private as it is going to get."

He sighed, his posture sagging in defeat. "Fine. I was talking to my friend Monica." He lowered his voice as Katie shushed him. "And she says you can intern for her in Dakota. However long you need to figure out decorating. She does residential as well as businesses. Homes, hotels, building lobbies, you name it."

"You called her on Christmas Day?" Who was this woman to him?

"Yes."

"Did you at least wish her a wonderful Christmas before asking a favor?"

"She's Jewish."

"I can't really afford to be an intern, but thank you for asking her."

"She would pay you well."

Katie couldn't meet his eyes. She hadn't shared her dream with anyone because she knew they'd then expect her to seize the day, make it happen, then skip off into the tastefully decorated sunset. All the while adding commentary on why she wasn't doing this, that or the other thing faster and better. Everyone would become an expert on her life, her career. But how could she make a living, picking out the right curtains to make a space feel homey? Who would pay for that sort of thing in Blueberry Springs? She'd have to leave everything: her hometown, her friends, her family, as well as a perfectly okay job.

All she wanted was to be happy. Was that too much to ask?

It probably wasn't, seeing as Nash was here to lift her onto the stepping stone between where she was and where she wanted to be.

The problem was, something like this would change her entire life.

"You could stay with me, or Monica, until you found a place. Take your time and add some experience, build a client base and then go out on your own."

"Quit pushing me," she whispered. This was just like with Beth. Nash had tried to make her into something she wasn't. And now he was trying to change Katie--make her become a decorator. And even though it was her dream to change careers, there were a lot of good reasons why Katie hadn't made that change on her own--and finding a place to intern wasn't one of them. Nash only saw the end result and not the hitches along the way. If she followed the path to decorating she would change herself as well as her entire life, and, frankly, she wasn't sure she was ready for that.

"I'm sorry." Nash pulled her close, hugging her with one arm. "I took it too far, too fast, didn't I? Grabbed your idea and ran with it, forgetting it was yours."

She nodded reluctantly. Now she felt like a big baby. He was trying to help and she was afraid to face change.

"Nursing isn't really that bad," she said.

"I didn't mean to scare you off."

"You didn't scare me off." Was this man a mind reader? Holy moly. She scooted out from under his arm. "And for your information, you don't determine me or my life."

"You should do this, Katie." He'd taken her slipping away to his advantage and faced her, grasping her arms. "You have what it takes."

"From what I've heard, I'm a good nurse, too."

"But does it still do it for you? Does it make you want to get out of bed each morning? Is it all you think about? Can you hardly wait to dive into each and every day? Do you lose yourself in it?"

"What about you? I thought your big dream was administration?"

He let go. "Beth told me I'd miss my patients, and she was right. I do." His expression clouded. "I've made many mistakes in my life, but you won't know if this is your real dream unless you chase it. What if there is something better out there for you?"

"Look, I've given it a lot of thought. It won't work, okay? It was only Mom's eggnog talking." Katie crossed her arms and backed down the hallway. "So let's drop it. It never happened."

"It wasn't the eggnog."

"You don't know squat." Katie hurried away, ticked that Nash was pursuing her.

"I know plenty and I know you aren't happy." He snagged her

arm, turning her to him, his free hand at her jaw. He tipped her head up, his eyes serious. It was just like in her romance novels.

She got it now. To have someone care enough to chase you down when you were upset. To not care if you got mad at them, because they needed to see you. To understand you. To show that you weren't alone.

Too bad it was Nash. A man who would be leaving in less than twenty-four hours.

"You need things your life isn't giving you, Katie." He lowered his mouth to hers and she sagged against him, knowing he could give her so many things. So many things.

But so many problems, too.

She pushed him away.

"What do you want from me, Nash? Am I just your new pet project?"

"No, Katie. You are the woman I've always needed."

Okay, she was going to swoon. He'd better be ready to catch her, because it was happening in three, two, one…

No, she was *not* going to swoon. He was totally the wrong guy, even though he was perfect in so many ways.

All the ways in which he wasn't perfect? He was trying to take over her life, as he had with Beth. He was leaving town tomorrow. He was Beth's ex. Katie's brother's arch rival. Her own nemesis. And he was a controlling perfectionist.

In other words, he was Nash.

She launched herself at him, banging him against the wall of the hospital hallway, her lips moving in a flurry over his warm skin. He lifted her up--man, he was strong--and turned so her spine was against the wall, her butt riding the narrow railing that ran along the corridor. His back was warm under her hands and his buttocks were a most excellent blend of firm and soft. Her body was tingling and she never wanted to let go.

"Well now," said a familiar voice, and Katie fell off the railing as Nash stepped back in surprise. She crashed against him, cheeks burning.

"Mary Alice," she croaked. "There's a blizzard out there."

The woman harrumphed, sending her large bosom lifting under her black snowmobile suit. "Give me some credit, kid." She brushed the skin near Katie's mouth. "You have some of Nash's tonsils on your cheek."

He laughed and Katie sent him a glare.

"Mary Alice." Nash gave the woman a hug.

Nash hugging Mary Alice? Okay, something was definitely up. Mary Alice and her sister, Liz, had practically run him out of town when he'd been chasing Beth. And when, weeks after the broken engagement and failed wedding, he'd gone back to the city, the sisters had all but dusted their hands and locked the town gates behind him. Not that the town had gates, but still, metaphorically speaking.

And now? The sisters were acting way too welcoming around Nash. It had to be more than his cologne setting them off. Cologne he seemed to not be wearing today.

Mary Alice released him and swung her snowmobile helmet jauntily. "Now, where is that father of yours, Katie?"

She inhaled sharply. Her father! He was still in the recovery room. Katie spun on her heel and took off, the squeak of Mary Alice's wet boots trailing behind her.

Pausing outside her father's door, Katie turned to Mary Alice. The woman unzipped her thick, one-piece snowsuit and plunged a hand down the neck of her fuzzy sweater. She fished around, her lips twisted in concentration. Her face brightened as she pulled an envelope from her cleavage. "I have a card for Harvey. Brownies, too. From Mandy's restaurant. Got them yesterday." She began exploring her cleavage again.

"Well, that's nice. Warm brownies. He'll like that." Katie fought her gag reflex at the thought of eating brownies warmed by Mary Alice's mega breasts. "It will be a few hours before he's up to eating. He just had surgery."

"It's the thought that counts. Did you know that when I had my hysterectomy last spring I went and saw Nash in the city? He made me feel so much better about it all. You don't need a womb to be a woman."

Katie shook the image of Mary Alice and Nash discussing reproductive parts from her mind. "That's…lovely."

"Did you know his ex-wife used to be a lawyer? Well, she still is, actually. Very nice lady. She's hoping he'll find someone nice to marry." Mary Alice gave Katie an assessing glance.

"That's great that they're still friends."

"Beth and Nash are, too, you know. Not all men can remain friends with an ex."

"Yeah, rather odd, huh? Well, here we are." She peeked into the recovery area, where her father was sleeping. "He's ready to go back to a regular room. Do you want to meet me in 107 in a few minutes?"

But Mary Alice followed her in, making herself at home. "What a place to spend Christmas. No offense to those who work here, but I mean, you understand…" She patted Katie's shoulder, then roused Harvey with a foot jiggle. "Hey, old man! What's the meaning of having appendicitis on your wife's big day, huh? Trying to get yourself killed? Angelica might be sweet and kind, but I don't doubt she'd take you out if amply motivated. We'd better get you home, pronto." Mary Alice waved a hand for Katie to help her as she began whipping blankets off him.

"He hasn't been cleared for anything but a regular room. He got out of the OR less than forty minutes ago." Katie grabbed the blankets back and flung them over the shivering man.

"I'm cold," her father said groggily. "Mary Alice, you look different."

"Oh? You like my hair?" She fluffed her short do and twisted her head from side to side.

"Maybe you could bring my mom here," Katie said, regretting the words as they left her mouth. "You managed to get through the snow. Wouldn't it be safer to try and bring Mom here instead of take Dad home?"

"Nonsense. I'm already here." Mary Alice lifted Harvey's arm and studied his IV. "How do you take one of these things out without making blood squirt everywhere?"

"I'll call security, Mary Alice," Katie warned. Nobody messed with Nurse Reiter and her orders. Not even Mary Alice.

"I want to go home," her father said. He struggled to sit up.

"Not a chance." She pushed her father back into a prone position. "Mary Alice…" Katie used her best warning voice.

Mary Alice lowered Harvey's arm and stared at her in shock. "Don't you go taking that tone with me." She lumbered over for a showdown. "And just so you know, Miss Katie Reiter, security isn't on tonight. Went home two hours ago. Had a nice rum and eggnog at your parents' place."

"Then I'll call Scott. He'll…arrest you." Katie winced. She was grasping at straws. Scott had never arrested a soul--not even Mandy, when he'd busted her spray painting her feelings for her best friend, Frankie, on the town's water tower. Apprehended her, yes. Arrested? Nope.

"I think he's consoling Amber, since her boyfriend, Russell, got stuck in the city." Mary Alice gave Katie a knowing look. "Again."

"She's not going to cheat on Russell. Mr. Book Deal is The One. Scott is just…he's…" He was a good friend who looked out for Amber. That was all. And yeah, maybe Scott still had a bit of a schoolboy crush on Amber, but that would never lead to anything between the two of them.

"Look, Mary Alice, you'll be endangering my father's life if you move him. There will be other Christmases."

"Not like this there won't." She turned to Harvey. "I'll bet you faked this attack, just like Katie *asked* to be put on the Christmas shifts." Mary Alice drew herself up, her snowsuit expanding in an alarming fashion. "You two might not respect the hard work that Angelica went to in order to ensure you have a good holiday season, but I, for one, will not stand here and allow you to ruin it!" The woman's eyes were damp.

Katie's adrenaline surged. Something was wrong. Really, terribly wrong.

"Mary Alice..." The soft words came from Nash. He walked slowly over and embraced her. To Katie's surprise, Mary Alice began sobbing.

He shushed her as he would a baby. Katie, unable to focus on anything else, watched in shock. Finally, she broke her spell by checking on her father. He was sleeping again. Quietly, she began prepping him for the move, hoping not to disturb the hugging duo.

This was another side of Nash she'd never seen before. He used to come across as cold and professional, but no more, and to mark the change, he was consoling one of the strongest women in town. More importantly, he knew whatever it was that was upsetting her.

Mary Alice had to be dying.

Heat flushed through Katie and she nearly fell over. What would Blueberry Springs be like without the woman? Mary Alice knew everyone and their business, and was there for the good, the bad, and the in between, always ready to help in the way she felt was best. And let's face it, in the case of Beth and Nash-- which everyone knew was a bad idea--hinder. She was the core of this town and without her they'd just be someplace out in the wilderness.

And speaking of wilderness, Jen Kulak, the nature guide who worked at Wally's Sporting Goods, was tracking massive amounts of snow through the halls as though all was right with the world. The woman paused and stared through the doorway, ski goggles half buried in her snow laden hat.

"Is there a doctor here today?" she asked.

"I'm a doctor." Nash released Mary Alice, who surreptitiously wiped her eyes.

"Who are you?" Jen inquired.

"Dr. Leham," Katie said. "He used to work here a few years back."

"Oh, right. Used to be engaged to Beth and all that. Well, I have an injured bird and couldn't get as far as the vet. Could you take a peek at it?"

"Where's your man, Jen?" asked Mary Alice. "Not out in the forest, is he?"

"Rob's shoveling the hospital walk. A ton of snow's come down already."

"How'd you get here?" Katie asked. She was fairly certain the outdoors hadn't turned to sunshine and rainbows in the ten minutes since she'd left the howling doorway.

"Snowshoes."

"Where is the bird?" Nash asked.

Katie sighed. Didn't anyone see how ridiculous this was? Everyone risking their lives in a blizzard?

"It flew into my window," Jen said. She glanced at Harvey. "Is that your dad? Is he okay?"

"Just had his appendix removed," Mary Alice interjected. "He's going home in a few minutes. I have my snowmobile out front. I just need to get him detached." She lifted the arm that had the IV. "Do you know how to unplug one of these things?"

Jen shook her head.

"Where's the bird?" Katie asked, nudging Nash toward Jen.

"It's in the lobby on a heat vent."

"Let's go take a look." Nash guided Jen out of the room, leaving Katie to face Mary Alice once again.

"A bird, huh? The world has gone crazy," Katie said, turning to her. The woman collapsed into a chair. "Are you okay?"

Mary Alice closed her eyes, her jaw tight. She was fighting it. Hard.

"I'm so sorry." Katie sat beside her.

"Not your fault. This is life. Do what we will with it. Time is limited. Cherish each moment. Eat your dessert first. Sing every song like nobody is watching. Or dance to it or whatever the stupid expression is." She placed her hands on her thighs and stood. "Let's get your father home."

"Mary Alice…"

"Nash said it would be okay."

"I'm pretty sure he didn't. Dad's barely even out of recovery."

"I wasn't talking about your father." Mary Alice jerked her snowsuit to straighten it. "Live a little, Katie. Jam-pack your days with something worthwhile that makes you smile. I'm tired of you holding back." Her voice was loud enough to wake Harvey. "You hear me? There is a perfectly good man kissing you like you are the only thing that can save his world, and you're standing here acting as though this is the life you want and the life you chose. Not to step on your toes, Harvey--" Mary Alice addressed the man, who was awake and interested "--but you chose her career, she didn't. You're good at it, Katie, but don't let that be the reason you stay in it. You hear me? Make your move."

"Katie is a good nurse," her father said.

"Mary Alice, you are going through a very emotional time--"

"Shut your yap. You know *nothing*." She yanked the IV out of Harvey's arm and he flinched, his face wrinkled in pain. Katie snatched a roll of gauze off a nearby stainless steel trolley and pressed it to the bleeding wound.

"You need to leave," she snapped. "Now!"

Mary Alice pointed a finger at her. "You pursue that man, you hear me?"

"Do it, Katie," her father said, his tone resigned.

"You're loopy from the anesthetic and don't know what you're talking about." Katie's throat was tight with tears.

Mary Alice went nose to nose with her. "Nash didn't come back just to say hi to old patients, or return a favor. He hoofed it out here when he heard you were single and would be on bare-bones shifts."

"You're..." *What? Crazy? Imagining things? Telling me exactly what I long to hear?*

"He's here for you," Mary Alice said with special emphasis.

"Balderdash."

"That's rather romantic," her father said.

"He's here for you," Mary Alice repeated. "So the question is, what are you going to do about it?"

5

What was she going to do about Nash? Her hands were sweating, her mind a mess. What if Mary Alice was wrong?

The woman was never wrong. What if she was *right*?

She had a connection with Nash that Katie hadn't expected. What if…

Don't think. That's all she had to do. Just shove all thoughts regarding Nash into the corner of her mind, along with being an interior decorator and Will ever asking her…no. *In the corner. Now stay there.*

Good. Great. It was Christmas. Be cheery.

She smoothed her ponytail, peeked down the quiet corridor, then shut the door to her father's new room. She'd convinced Mary Alice that Harvey would perk up if she got him a cup of coffee, sending the woman to the cafeteria while she rolled her father into a room close enough to the nursing station that she could keep an eye on him. For good measure, she'd locked him to the bed.

He was asleep again and anyone trying to jailbreak him was bad news for his life expectancy. Full stop. She was doing what security would do if they actually had hauled their butt in for a full day of work. Well, no, actually. They would have kicked Mary Alice out, but quite frankly, Katie didn't think she had it in her.

She glanced at the clock. Time for a little bit of Christmas cheer. Not carols over the PA, that was too Angelica Reiter and she wasn't going down that road. But Katie had a box of Christmas cookies from Mandy that she could share with the six or so patients who were in their rooms, and then the five continuing-care patients who hadn't gone home to their families for the holiday.

Katie pulled the lid off the tin and inhaled the buttery sweetness of the shortbread cookies. Too tempting. She stole a small square and popped it in her mouth. What was it about Mandy that made her so awesome at baking? No wonder her restaurant was doing so well, her desserts were devilishly divine. Katie sneaked a second cookie, savoring the way it melted in her mouth. Nothing better in the world. And likely nothing better for adding girth to her hips. She tucked a third cookie in her mouth and smiled.

Who cared? She was single. May as well enjoy the perks.

She walked through the double doors to the continuing care nursing home attached to the hospital as Elsie Nagorski trudged by, her long grey hair swept up in a high bun.

"Still not dancing?" Katie asked, following the woman into her room. It had been months since Elsie had stopped dancing her way to and fro through the continuing care area, but it still felt odd.

"I will never dance again. All the good celebrities are dying. It makes me feel *old*. All my contemporaries are knocking off, calling it a day, pushing up daisies from six feet under."

"Right." Depressing. But not a lot she could do on that one. "So? What are you up to today? Anything good on TV?"

Elsie's eyes lit up and she clasped her hands together in front of her flowered housedress. "Yes! You know Hailey Summer, the girl I told you about from Muskoka?"

"Yes. Right. I met her once."

"Well, she's with a movie star now. I *told* my sister, Wilma Star, that it really was Hailey with him last summer. Didn't I? I did." She gave a decisive nod. "She still owes me five dollars. She's as cheap as the day is long. In Alaska. During the summer equinox. That cheap." Another nod.

"I'll remind her if I see her." Katie moved to the figurine shelf where Elsie had princesses on display. One was out of line and she straightened it, positioning it with the rest.

"Thanks, dear. That one has been bothering me, but with this shoulder..."

"Do you need anything?"

"No," Elsie gave a dejected sigh and took her spot in front of her aging television. "Commercials are over."

"Is that Hailey?" Katie asked, peering at the screen. The woman was beaming from the TV, wrapped in the embrace of a movie star. Finian Alexander. My, he was an eyeful of yum.

"It is. They are doing a charity thing. It's very cute. They're fixing Finian's old neighbourhood." Elsie wiped a tear from a damp eye. "You need to find yourself a man like that and save the world, Katie. It needs it so much."

"I think your dancing problems are solved. Dance for Mr. Alexander here." Katie resisted fanning herself. "I'm going to continue my rounds. Buzz me if you need anything, Mrs. Nagorski. Dinner in the common area at six."

"It always is."

"I asked Leif from Benny's to bring you a nice slice of roast beef."

"Oh, Katie. You are such a dear. You really are the best. Just like your father says."

"He doesn't say that when I argue with him."

She left Elsie and turned into Beth's grandmother's room,

inhaling the scent of her powdery, floral perfume *Love Chloé* that hung in the air, expecting the suite to be empty.

"Gran! I thought Beth was taking you home?"

"Oz needed her to run an errand, and she didn't want to leave me waiting in the cold car. Said she'd be back later, but now there's a blizzard." The elderly woman heaved a mighty sigh.

"I'm stuck here, too." Katie offered the tin of cookies, and Gran began to shake her head. "Mandy made them."

She took two. "Thanks, dear. I think I'll have a nip of sherry to go with it. Borski-Nagorski--"

"Borski?"

"She's been boring everyone with her video chats. Like we didn't hear and see it all with her in the common room, nattering so loudly with her sister over in Muskoka. Her friend's daughter and that boyfriend of hers. You would think she was the first person to get in bed with a movie star. I need a drink, dear."

"Lucky woman, that Hailey."

"Speaking of getting lucky...pass the sherry?" Gran asked hopefully. She pointed behind Katie to a bottle sitting by framed photos of Beth and her sister, Cynthia, both of whom Gran had raised. "Nash, bless his heart, brought me some of the finer stuff."

"He's changed, don't you think?" He was sweeter. Dreamier.

Gran waved a paper pill cup she'd dug out of the trash by her recliner. "Just a finger. How is your father? I heard he's in."

Katie poured her a shot. "Appendicitis. He's recovering well. You can visit if you'd like." She capped the bottle. "I've got to go check on a few others. Buzz me if you need anything, okay?"

"I may fake arrhythmia later. Nash's tush is a sight for sore eyes."

Katie released another burst of laughter. "I don't think anyone would blame you." She struggled to blink away visions of his tush in the nude.

Gran knocked back the shot and held out the cup, wiggling it until she filled it again. "You seem different, Katie."

"It's the holiday getup." She gestured to her garb, knowing Gran had caught her faraway, dreamy look.

"Not what I meant and you know it."

Katie placed the bottle back where she'd found it and hightailed it into the hall. Finishing her quick round, she headed to her station.

"Katie?" The voice was familiar, kind, and hesitant. Her ex.

Couldn't be.

Yes, could be. Was.

"Doesn't anyone listen to the weatherman and stay home in a blizzard?" she asked, turning to face him.

"I wanted to see you." The distance between them was being eaten up at a great rate. They were both moving. His hands were extended; hers were lifting to meet them despite her desire to push him away.

Was this the moment?

Was it?

If it was, why didn't she feel more excited? More like her life was finally going to lift off?

A patient alarm went off at Katie's desk and she turned back, thankful for the distraction. She reached over the counter and connected to the room in question. "Yes?"

"Merry Christmas, honey." It was her dad. "Say, I was just thinking…have I been arrested? I seem to be…" He paused as he searched for the right word.

"You aren't to go anywhere, understand? Sit tight."

"Nature seems to be calling my name in a rather loud voice."

"You have a catheter." Thankfully, Amy had done that pre-op, but the nurse had yet to remove it. Where was she, anyway? Katie hadn't seen Amy since the operation. Hopefully, she hadn't decided to go home, since her shift was over. There was no way Katie wanted to go anywhere near her father's family jewels. Nursing degree or no nursing degree.

"I…"

"Dad, just let it rip. In fact, you probably already have. It's a catheter and it--"

"No. The other kind."

Oh, sweet mother of... Katie closed her eyes and thought for a moment. Yes, this was indeed proportionally worse than being at her parents' house and dealing with holiday overload. Served her right.

"I'll send Amy in shortly, okay?" She hung up the phone, paged Amy to her father's room and turned to Will. "Not really a great time right now. I'm working."

"I know."

He wanted something. She could tell. He had that hitch in his shoulders like he did when he wasn't sure if she was going to yell at him.

"What do you need?" she asked.

"You." He dropped to one knee and Katie's heart nearly gave out.

"Stand up!" He couldn't do this. Not right here. Not now.

"Not one of these again," Gran said, and turned back toward the continuing-care wing. "Christmas proposals are so overdone. I'll visit Harvey later."

"Kathryn Jane Reiter, I have loved you since the day you told me my shirt was stained and you passed me your stain-remover pen."

He was holding her hand really tightly. His grip was sweaty and Katie feared her fingers would suddenly come flying out of his. She kind of hoped they would.

No, wait. She wanted him to hold her hand. She wanted this. She'd been expecting it.

She smiled.

Finally.

How things were supposed to be.

"You are the woman who matches me." Wasn't he so sweet? They were right for each other and he could see it, too. "You make sure my socks are the same and my colors coordinate. You wash my clothes and take good care of me."

Come to think of it, his Dockers were looking a tad grubby. And he obviously hadn't ironed them. This man needed her.

"You are everything I'm not, Katie Reiter."

Yes, that was likely true.

Movement beyond Will caught her eye and Katie glanced up. Nash paused, took in the scene, then quietly backed out of the corridor, his head bent over the shoe box he was carrying.

The floor tilted under Katie's feet. Something wasn't right.

This was wrong.

She blinked down at Will, the man she'd loved for years.

"You are my perfect match. You are my…" He was still talking about her as if she were his mother and maid all rolled into one.

Katie hefted him to his feet. "Look, Will. I don't think I'm your match, and, honestly, us trying to make each other into the person we want is exhausting."

He frowned.

"It is. Okay? This isn't going to happen. Not for us. Not today. Sorry."

She fled into a nearby storage closet, slamming the door so hard a flurry of damp mops fell on top of her as she collapsed into a sobbing heap.

The supply closet door cracked opened a few minutes later, allowing a shaft of light and a powdery scent to enter. Gran.

Unable to hold in the sobs, Katie felt her body shake and her humiliation rise like Benny's blood pressure when he cooked with too much salt. What she wouldn't do for a slice of his Chocolate Maven pie right now. She dropped her chin onto her knees and held her breath, struggling to trap the emotions that had broken free.

"Katie dear?" The warmth of the old woman's body pressed into her side as she joined her on the floor.

"Oh, don't sit," Katie wailed. "We'll never get you up again."

Gran laughed good-naturedly. "Probably not. But I happen to know ol' blue eyes is in the building and will help me out."

"Frank Sinatra?" That was the only ol' blue eyes she knew. "Is it time for another mental test, Gran?"

The woman chuckled. "Nash Leham."

Katie sighed. He *was* crush worthy, wasn't he?

Gran snuggled in, making herself comfortable in the crowded closet. "Now, what's all this about? Did you say no to poor William?"

Katie sniffed and nodded, but realizing Gran couldn't see her in the dark, she let out a plaintive "Yeah."

"Are you regretting that choice already?"

Katie thought about it. "No."

"Then you must be worried about his feelings?"

"Not really."

"Then what's the fuss?"

"I thought this was what I wanted. I've been imagining this moment for weeks, and now...and I said no and...and I don't know what my life is anymore." Her inhalation turned to hiccups.

Gran hugged her closer. "Oh, dear."

"I mean, this is what women want. What I want. A great job that they are good at, a man who loves them and wants to marry them. And I'm saying no to it all."

Outside in the corridor, Christmas carols began, and a new round of sobs welled up within Katie.

"Is this about someone else?"

"No."

"It's Nash Leham, isn't it?" Gran asked, her voice tight. "He's doing it again."

"He's not doing anything. And he didn't break up Beth and Oz, Gran. He made them stronger, because without him going after Beth, Oz wouldn't have got his act together."

"You like him."

Katie stood, patting around for the light switch. She flicked it on and winced.

The door opened and Mary Alice stared in. Beyond her, Harvey sat in a wheelchair, looking pleased with himself. "I'm taking your father home."

"I feel great. Invincible!" Her dad raised a hand as though wielding a sword.

"It's the drugs." Katie carefully helped Gran off the floor, tears threatening. "You need to stay here. You just had surgery."

"I'm going home."

"He's fine," Mary Alice said. "He's going home."

"Fine. I quit."

"What?" all three asked her.

Katie closed her eyes, breath held in. That was not supposed to come out. She slowly opened her eyes and exhaled. "I quit. I'm moving to the city to intern as an interior decorator." She waited as the stunned expressions turned to ones of confusion.

Mary Alice swung a fist through the air, her bulky suit rustling with the action. "I knew it!"

"You did not," Katie snapped.

"Okay, I didn't." She gave her a Cheshire cat grin. "But I suspected you were up to something big. Maybe you should take a nursing job in Dakota, so you have some money while you intern. I'll ask Nash to give you a reference."

"I'm done nursing," Katie said softly.

"Near cleaned me out with that degree and now she doesn't want it?" Harvey muttered. "Is this real? Am I dreaming?"

"Nursing was your choice, Dad, not mine."

"What's wrong with you kids?" he asked, his voice rising. "I get you good jobs so you can support yourselves, a family, and you don't want them!"

Tears brimmed in his eyes and Katie felt as big as an aphid. She tipped her chin up. "Yeah, well, merry Christmas. Tell Mom I said hi."

KATIE HUDDLED AWAY from the flurry of icy flakes stinging her skin. How had so many people made it in through this storm? She couldn't see anything five feet from her snowy bench. Her feet were numb and her fingers hurt so bad she could scream.

But nobody would bother her in the hospital's smoke pit, where she'd fallen into a personal pit of despair. She'd told the one person she shouldn't--Mary Alice. The news about her changing her life was probably already all over town. Blizzards couldn't slow a swarm of gossip locusts.

Just. Like. That.

Her whole life had changed.

Katie plunged her head into her hands, then sagged against the bench's snowy backrest. A clump of snow fell off the bush behind her, going down the neck of her coat. She gasped at the cold and tried to fish the chunk out with frozen fingers.

Her life had been fine less than forty-eight hours ago. And now it was... Well, whatever it was, it was Nash's fault. If it weren't for him, she would have said yes to Will. If it weren't for Mary Alice, she wouldn't be thinking about Nash. If it weren't for Nash, she wouldn't be thinking about changing careers. If it weren't for...oh, who was she kidding? She hadn't been happy in so long she couldn't even remember what true joy felt like.

She hadn't been unhappy, but she hadn't had that twinkle-in-the-eye, heart-lifting exuberant love for life in so long, she wasn't sure it was still possible.

She was like Beth had been when Oz had dumped her.

Exactly like Beth.

Then Nash had come in, shaken everything up and left again. He'd changed Beth's life irrevocably. For the better. And then Beth went back to Oz.

There was no way Katie was going back to Will. She'd refused him. Beth had never refused Oz. Not like this.

Tears blazed stinging trails down Katie's frozen cheeks.

The door beside her creaked open, the hydraulics unhappy with the subzero temperature.

"Katie?"

Nash. Of course.

"You okay?"

"Peachy."

"Mary Alice said you're quitting?" There was a hitch of disbelief in his voice.

"Looks like it." There was that swarm, doing its work. "So, what's wrong with her?"

"Mary Alice? Nothing a little medical attention won't fix."

"She's not dying?"

"Not today. However, I doubt she is truly invincible. She does believe it's her time to go, though. Patients are usually wrong about that when it is their first brush with mortality."

The relief Katie felt was unexpected, and tears began in earnest. "I have to change my life." She sobered up suddenly. Too much crying. Enough wallowing in self-pity. It was time to form a new life plan.

What was she thinking? Her former life plan had trapped her in a career she wasn't passionate about, and hoping a man she didn't love would ask her to become his wife.

Although, possibly it wasn't the plan as much as her focusing on it too much. She should have checked to see what could be added or deleted from it every so often, as things--including herself--changed. She hadn't even seriously considered what else was out there for her and how she could get it.

"What are you going to do?" Nash asked gently, as he tucked a blanket from the warmer over her lap. How long had he been watching her wallow out here, trying desperately to pull the unraveling threads of her existence back together? Her life was a sock that could not be darned, the weave too worn and loose to be mended. She needed to start over. Weave her own sock, one that would be strong enough to contain her real life. A life that could be bigger.

Katie stood, letting the heated blanket fall into the snow. Her legs felt the chill immediately, making her regret standing. "I'm going to… I'm going to…" She stared into the white space behind Nash. The wind had suddenly died, the flakes turning fatter. Beautiful. Sparkling as the sun strived to sneak through a break in the storm.

Nash appeared in front of her and she blinked to focus on him instead.

"You okay?" He shivered, hands clutched in front of him. He wasn't wearing a coat or gloves and there was a layer of snow on his blond hair. His nose and cheeks had turned an alarming shade of red.

"Yeah, fine. Let's go inside."

"It's a gong show in there. If you want to talk, let's do it here."

"You're freezing."

"I feel as though I've tossed your world upside down. Gran is giving me dirty looks…I'm guessing you didn't say yes to Will?"

Katie sighed, her chest tight with a trapped hiccup.

"I don't want today to come between us," he added.

"Nash…" Katie shifted awkwardly, not meeting his eyes. Her feet were in danger of frostbite, as was most of him.

He cupped her face with his icy hands. "Katie, shh. It's okay." He placed his mouth against hers, the coldness shocking. As they kissed, their lips warmed, and Katie was unable to resist wrapping her arms around him, even when it made her coat dip down, exposing the damp skin on the nape of her neck where the snow had melted. It was worth it.

The door creaked open. "Really? Him? You said no for *him?*" Will gave Katie a disgusted glare and stormed past, looking ridiculous when he tried to wade through the waist-deep snow.

"Will. You can't go out in this. It's too dangerous."

"Up yours, Katie!"

"Will! It's not safe. Come back here. I don't want the plow finding your frozen body in the morning."

"I'll make sure to die where it can't find me."

"Will. Come on."

"You aren't the boss of me!" He continued to wade through the snow, scrambling up a hard drift fifteen feet away, which proved to be Katie's car. Lovely. Good luck driving home before spring thaw.

Nash shook his head, more amused than anything. "I can't kiss you anywhere, can I?"

Mary Alice zipped by on her snowmobile and stopped beside Will. "Look at that sunshine!" she hollered. She gestured to the seat behind her and he climbed on.

"Where's my dad?" Katie called over the whine of the snow machine.

"I'm picking him up at the other door. Amy's got him ready."

"Did you release him?" Katie asked, turning to Nash.

He scratched his ear. "Kind of."

"Are you kidding me?"

"You'll be there, right? That's what Mary Alice said." He tucked his hands in his armpits and hunched his shoulders. "Plus, I was invited over for supper."

"He could…he's…" Katie sighed. "Whatever." She turned and went inside, the heater above the door blasting her with dry heat that made her frozen skin prickle.

Nash followed her in. "Katie?"

"What?" She continued walking.

"Are you moving to the city?"

"Why?"

"Mary Alice said you're moving to the city, and I'd like to see you. Take you out for dinner. Or if you'd like, you could stay with me while you intern."

"Nash…" Katie whirled. "I was spouting off, okay? Eggnog talking. I haven't even spoken to your friend Monica."

"You're drinking on the job?"

"I'm kidding. I'm flustered. I just threw my life against the windshield of a speeding truck."

He was doing that close-in-on-her thing where suddenly you found yourself trapped. But his eyes were kind and she sort of wanted him to trap her. Why? Because this man saw the real Katie. The one everyone else scoffed at for liking stain-free clothes. And he wanted to break her free so she could frolic in her own fields for a while.

"I can wait. I've already waited two years," he told her.

"What are you talking about?"

"You. Us."

Whoops. Knees kind of weakened a bit there. Did he just say that? Really?

Man, he was good.

"I've always been here," she whispered.

"You were taken. And despite what you think of me, I don't steal another man's woman." His right hand caressed her cold cheek. She wanted to curl into his grasp, warm herself on him and whatever he was offering.

"What are you saying, Nash?"

"I want you, Katie. You and me. We're like oil and vinegar, but in a good way." She frowned and he smiled. A soft one. He brought his forehead to hers. "Like bread-dipping oil. A touch of red wine vinegar, extra virgin olive oil, and a few herbs."

"Who are you calling a virgin?"

His smile stretched. "And, honestly, I could do without those herbs poking about." His eyes flicked to the door they'd just come through.

"Yeah," she replied softly. "Me, too."

"Just us. Me and you."

That settled the emotions whirling within Katie. *Us.*

Never a better sounding word in the world.

6

Katie finished helping patients with their Christmas dinner, while aching for her family. She didn't expect to want to be home with them for the big meal, but knowing that even her father had made it to enjoy everyone's home-cooked favorites sucked. Her mother had called a few minutes ago to let her know that he was doing just fine.

Katie was off shift in fifteen minutes, and the snow had let up, but she didn't think she could get out of here, even if the relief shift made it in.

Nash sidled up beside her and held out her cell phone. "It was ringing. I thought it might be important."

"Thanks." Katie glanced at number of the call she'd missed. Mary Alice. Whatever. The woman wasn't dying, according to Nash, so she didn't get immunity in terms of telling the whole world Katie was quitting her job. Helping her surprised and upset patients for the past hour had not been fun. They seemed to believe Katie was going to run out on them without giving them their turkey or meds.

"You heading home in fifteen?" Nash asked.

Katie sighed and returned to her station. "I don't think I'm going anywhere until the plows come in the morning."

"I heard one working on the ambulance bay a few minutes ago."

"Really?" Katie perked up, before the sting of disappointment seized her as she realized the residential streets she'd need would likely still be impassable--assuming she could even get her car out. Her other option was to wade through waist-deep, frozen fluff for a half mile. Not worth it. Not even for her mother's amazing mashed potatoes made with cream and butter.

Nash cocked his head, and without thinking, Katie fell against him, wanting to be close, needing him to reassure her.

"You're strange," she said, as he wrapped her in an embrace that filled her heart with smiles.

"Why's that?" He craned his neck to see her face.

"Because." She bit her bottom lip, unable to express that around him she felt stronger. But at the same time, she was able to let her vulnerable side show, knowing he'd protect it with his strength. Not like with Will. If she showed her soft underbelly to him, the whole world would devolve into chaos and a big whine-fest. With Nash, it was as though he could take that worry and fear, and mold and shape it with his presence until it became one of her own strengths.

How had he ever been her enemy?

"Keep your friends close and your enemies closer," she whispered.

Nash held her away from him. "Am I still your enemy?"

"You made me tell Mary Alice I was quitting."

"I kept your secret."

"I know." She snuggled in, her body melting against his again. "And you're not really my enemy."

"Good." He disentangled himself and began walking away, and Katie felt as though she'd hurt a good friend.

"What?" she called.

"I'll catch you later. I have to do something."

Yeah, go home to the city. Where she was going to go, as well. Maybe. Oh, boy. Deep breath. "Hey! Didn't you say you had a gift for me? And you never thanked me for the box of chocolates I gave you yesterday."

He didn't answer.

Men. So confusing.

Katie sorted through papers on her desk, thinking about how it felt as though Nash had shuffled her life into the proper order over the past two days. Almost as if her earlier life had been one of those flip-a-card games where she had the body of nurse, a clown's head, and stockinged legs with heels. Only Nash had flipped through the cards to show her what the real Katie Reiter looked like.

She finished her shift and went to visit Gran, who fell asleep after looking at a few pages of her family photo album. Katie jumped when the relief nurse, Hillary, tapped her shoulder.

"Oh! You scared me," Katie said, quietly shutting the book.

"I hear you're leaving us to go become a decorator?"

She rolled her eyes. "It's just a rumor. I might, though, but nothing is for sure."

"Well, I think you'd be great at it. When you decorated the nurses' station for the holidays, you knew just the right amount of cheer to place there."

"Thanks."

"And the staff room. The paint color you picked out is perfect. It goes nicely with the furniture."

"Thanks."

"And the way you redid Will's place years ago. I heard that was quite nice. Sort of like one of those reality shows? You know, while you were out shopping we redid your house. Do you think you'll be on one of those?"

"Hillary..." Katie said, feeling impatient.

She clapped a hand to her mouth. "Oh! I'm so sorry. I forgot you turned Will down. I was so surprised. You kept saying he was going to ask you back. Are you making him wait, for dumping you just before Christmas? I know you have that big stereo for him." She clamped a palm over her mouth once more. "You returned it? Oh no! Definitely make him wait until after the holidays. Then you don't have to go buy it back again."

"No, I just don't think we are well matched."

"That's what your father said." Hillary mimicked a deep male voice. "Will is a nice guy, but not the right guy."

"When did he say that?"

"When I stopped by to admire your mom's decorations earlier. Christmas dinner smelled so good." She checked her watch. "You'd better get moving. Angelica said she'd hold the meal for you."

Katie stood. "She did?"

Hillary walked her to the staff room so she could get her coat, while getting the rundown on how the day shift had been. Uneventful other than her father.

"He looked fine, by the way," Hillary said. "I took his vitals when I stopped in for some eggnog on my way here. And with you staying the night--you are staying at your mom's and not going to try and get home after supper?" She waited for Katie to respond.

Coat zipped, Katie stared out at the dark parking lot. The streetlights made the snow look beautiful, all crystals and white drifts of indeterminable depths. How was she going to get out?

"Yeah, I guess I'll stay in my old room. Johnny Depp on the walls…. He's probably lonely," she said, mostly to herself. Was she supposed to have redecorated the room when she moved out? Or was her mother that afraid to let go? Thinking her girl might need a place to land and want her old high school movie star crush to be there to catch her?

"Well, have a good night. Merry Christmas." Hillary turned and walked away, leaving Katie wondering how on earth she was going to get her car out from under that mound of snow, and then somehow plow her way across town to her parents' place sometime before the New Year. She couldn't even tell where the roads were.

The whine of a snowmobile grew louder and Katie prepped herself for an emergency. Instead, Mary Alice pulled up, lumbered through the snow and wrenched open the door.

"You coming or what?"

"Or what," Katie snapped.

"Shut up." Mary Alice tugged on her arm, reminding her of the one time she'd tried shoplifting, and had gotten caught. Worst. Day. Ever. Having Mary Alice take a round out of her and then hand her off to her parents, so they could take another round out of her.

"Your folks are expecting you." The woman shoved a helmet at Katie's gut. "Your mother sent this."

Katie climbed on behind Mary Alice, secretly grateful. The helmet was warm and a bit too big. Mary Alice didn't start the machine moving, and Katie followed her line of vision. A man in the hospital doorway. Big coat. Big boots. Alone.

Christmas.

Crap.

"Are you coming?" Katie called to Nash. She swore Mary Alice nodded in approval.

Without a word, he pushed through the snow and climbed on behind Katie.

"Can it take us all, Mary Alice?" he asked over the roar of the engine. His voice in Katie's ear, his body wrapped around hers…shiverama.

She was starting to like winter storms. A lot.

ANGELICA DISHED an extra large scoop of mashed potatoes onto

Nash's plate and beamed at him. "Thank you for joining us tonight."

"Thank you for having me, Mrs. Reiter."

"Dear…" From her spot at the table's end, opposite her husband, she reached to tap Nash's hand. "Call me Angelica. Please."

Sitting beside Nash, Katie shifted, trying to avoid her sister-in-law's questioning gaze. The aromas of warm turkey, spices, and the cranberry-scented candles lining the long table battled to calm her edgy nerves. She enjoyed having Nash here; that wasn't the problem. It was her father, who was seated to her left. He should be in the hospital. He should be eating Jell-O, not a heavy meal.

"Everyone got here okay?" Katie asked mildly, avoiding meeting Beth's eye. "The snow wasn't too bad?"

"We live three houses away." Oz flicked a pea at her, eliciting a giggle from his toddler son, Benji, who in turn threw a handful at his grandfather. The boy gave a giant laugh, his high chair rocking, as Harvey sent him a stunned look.

"How are you feeling, Dad?" Katie asked.

"Fine. And I have the best nurse and doctor in town at my table. What could go wrong?"

She held her breath. No comment about her quitting? Really?

"I heard a rumor," her mother began tentatively.

Katie watched her father eye the turkey. "You shouldn't be eating solid food, Dad. Maybe we could put your meal in Benji's baby food blender? Beth do you still have it?"

Her father shot her a disgusted look.

"I lent it out," Beth replied. "Sorry."

"Have you had a BM post-op? Any gas?" Katie asked her father.

"Please," Angelica said, pressing a palm against the red tablecloth. "No bowel movement discussions at the table."

"What?" Katie's indignation rose along with her anxiety. "Oz and Beth are always talking about Benji's, and Dad just had major surgery. If he eats this stuff he could paralyze his bowel."

Nash nudged her elbow. "It's okay." To Harvey, he said, "Just stick to the mashed potatoes and gravy for now and you should be fine." His eyes were warm and reassuring, and Katie relaxed despite her fears. Despite…everything.

"Whoa!" Oz pushed back from the table, hands held high, eyes wide in shock. "Did my sister just take a chill pill?" He grinned as she glowered at him, then he leaned forward, elbows on the table, fork poised for food stabbing. Seriously, did he not learn from Mom how to hold a fork like a gentleman? Nash held his properly. Linen napkin placed over his lap. Using the right utensil. Why couldn't he be her family?

Well. That was a thought. Nash *could* be family.

"I think you just did," Oz said, shoveling a wad of stuffing into his grinning mouth.

"Is it warm in here?" Katie asked. Things were definitely heating up under her sweater.

"Hmm. I think that really did happen," Beth said with a glimmer of a smile. "Katie chilled out."

"Shut up. It's the wine." She took another glug of her mulled drink and handed the empty glass to Nash, so her mother could top it up.

"You did a fine job on me today," Harvey said to Nash. "Thank you, son."

"Son?" Oz choked.

"The rumor I heard was that you got a marriage proposal today," Angelica said, turning to Katie.

Beth stood, her chair flying back. "Ohmigod. Show me your hand!"

Oz snatched his wife's water glass from her belly's danger zone as she impatiently reached across the table.

Katie held up her bare finger.

"Making him work for it, are you?" her brother asked, with a sigh and a shake of his head. "My sister will die an old maid."

Katie lowered all but her middle finger and glared at him.

"What happened?" Beth asked softly.

Katie could feel Nash, who had been leaning farther away from her, his body tight at the mention of her proposal, soften.

She shrugged. "Could you pass the gravy, please?"

"Turkey or beef?" her mother replied.

"You made both?"

"Of course I did."

Katie glanced at the table. "This is a ridiculous amount of food, Mom."

"I was expecting Beth's grandmother, sister, and brother-in-law." Angelica's mouth formed a tight line.

"I'm sorry," Beth said.

"You're not Mother Nature, now are you? Turkey gravy will go best." Angelica passed the antique gravy boat that had graced their table for eons.

"How long are you in town?" Oz asked Nash.

"Oz, give him a break," Katie said.

"I thought you two didn't like each other," her brother said.

"We got over it."

Oz stood, his face dark. He was doing an alarming amount of back-and-forth sizing up between her and Nash.

"Shut up and eat your supper," Katie muttered.

"Good advice," their father said, raising an eyebrow at his son.

Oz flung down his linen napkin. Then, with his jaw set, he slumped back into his chair, his arm slung around Beth's shoulders.

"That Will was a nice fellow, Katie," Harvey said.

"Yes. I believe he still is," she replied.

"But he wasn't the right man for you. You can do better."

"Any suggestions for her?" Beth asked playfully.

Everyone but Oz glanced at Nash, and Katie resisted the urge to slide under the table and never come out.

"So? Everyone get what they want for Christmas?" she asked, after clearing her throat.

"Not yet," Nash replied under his breath. He gave her a look so loaded with meaning that her stomach did a flip and her cheeks burned with anticipation of what he might be thinking.

Things were getting hot in here, that was for sure.

SHE PROBABLY SHOULDN'T BE MAKING out with Nash in the pantry under the stairs. But his lips were *so* good.

And yeah, her pissed-off brother and his wife--Nash's ex-fiancée, aka Katie's BFF, aka Katie's sister-in-law--were cluelessly playing with their son in the living room, which put a tiny bit of a damper on things when Katie thought about it.

So she didn't think about it.

Which was quite easy, seeing as Nash was a killer with those lips of his. All she had to do was tip her head back, wrap her arms around his strong shoulders and go along for the ride. A hot and heavy feeling settled in her gut and she wound a leg around Nash's hips. In the process her foot bumped a stack of cans on a shelf, sending them banging to the floor.

Nash let out a pained squawk, which was stifled against Katie's mouth.

They stilled, listening for approaching footsteps. Either everyone knew the two were making out in here or they were deaf as could be.

Right.

Cue up forthcoming awkward and embarrassing moment, multiplied by the number of family members on the other side of the door. Katie should straighten her Rudolph sweater, head out there with a dusty can of green beans from the back of the pantry and declare that they'd found them at long last. Assuming her lipstick wasn't smeared all across her face. She was pretty sure it was, actually.

She grabbed Nash, surprised at how soft his perfect, short hair was as she added another kiss to their growing history. His hands ran up her back, skating in circles as he explored the way their bodies fit together. And that? How they fit together? Awesome. Completely and utterly. With Will it was as though there was always an extra hand in the mix or their lips didn't quite match up properly. But with Nash…it was like in her romance novels. Real life could mimic her favorite books with this man against her lips. And how incredible was that? It made her want to do wild and crazy things to see if she could play out a whole three-hundred-page love story with her hunk.

The pantry door whipped open, spilling light into the enclosed space.

"Are you two for real?" Beth stared at them, her eyes brimming with tears. "Don't you know I'm pregnant and can't take this kind of…of…"

Nash was at Beth's side in a flash, consoling her, as Katie fought off the sting of being second fiddle. Maybe she should start crying, to see if he'd come to her side. He was the man Katie wanted. He wasn't Beth's--why couldn't they see that?

Wait. Stop that train before it hurtled off the tracks and hurt someone. Nash was *not* the man she wanted.

"Sorry," she said curtly. "Mistletoe." She pointed to the garland her mother had strung around the pantry's small door frame. Walking away, Katie smoothed her sweater, pivoting into the main floor washroom to assess the lipstick damage, so she wouldn't murder her best friend for snagging Nash's attention so easily.

THERE WAS STOMPING on the front porch where Oz had cleared a small patch, so people could come and go without a foot or two of snow falling into the entry whenever the door opened. Katie, who had been avoiding everyone by hiding elbow-deep in sudsy water as she tackled her mother's worst pots and pans, went to the door, hoping her family--and Nash--remained downstairs, where they were checking out her father's new flooring.

Katie wiped her hands on a Christmas tree tea towel, peeked out the lace curtain on the small quarter window and almost laughed at how her mom's lit-up lawn ornaments were leaving eerie glowing patches of evil red and green under the mounds of fresh snow. Very festive indeed.

She opened the door to let in her friends Mandy and Amber.

"Merry Christmas."

"Merry Christmas," they chorused, leaving their snowshoes outside.

Mandy handed Katie a small white bag containing her special whiskey and gumdrop brownies. Heaven and sin all wrapped into one chocolaty tidbit.

"I'll never fit in my scrubs ever again."

"From what I hear that won't be necessary, and besides, don't they have those fashionable elastic waistbands?" Mandy pushed back the hood of her coat, her hair a smooth gloss that wasn't at all affected by being shoved under a static-inducing layer of cold protection. How did the woman do it? It felt as if everyone had wonderful hair except Katie. Hence the ubiquitous ponytails.

"Ah, the rumor mill is alive and well, then."

"As always."

"So? You two doing it yet?" Amber asked, draping her insulated army surplus jacket over the nearby banister.

"Don't even go there."

"It's that bad? Huh. I would have thought with the way you growl whenever anyone mentions him that it would be crazy-hot in bed."

Katie took Mandy's coat, ignoring Amber.

"Frankie's over at his aunt's place clearing off her back porch, so her dog can get out to do his business," Mandy said. "Amber and I figured we'd pop in. Any eggnog left?"

"Russell got snowed in," Amber said moodily. "Can't make Christmas."

"I thought he sold his novel. Why was he in the city?" Katie asked. "Eggnog's in the kitchen."

"Promo stuff," Amber replied. "And getting ready for the launch in March."

"He's been in the city a lot," Mandy said. Katie nodded. Lately, spotting the couple together was as tricky as confirming a Sasquatch sighting.

"I miss him," Amber said with a sad sigh. "But the reunion sex is amazing. It's almost worth him being away so much." She took a candy cane from the entry's side table and bit off a chunk.

"Yeah, okay. Let's talk about something else, shall we?" Katie said brightly. There was one thing she didn't need and that was Amber talking about her sex life. Ever. Her friend had a way of sharing way too much information, and there were some things Katie didn't want to imagine.

Mandy cast a glance at Benji, curled up fast asleep in Harvey's armchair, as they passed the quiet living room to join Amber at the cookie table. "Such a cutie. By the way, I heard Nash was over?"

"He's downstairs with my parents and the gang."

Mandy rubbed her hands together. "Getting the first degree from Oz then? How does Beth feel about him proposing to you?"

"What?" Katie dropped the tea towel, then swooped it up, praying her cheeks weren't flushing like mad. "No. Will proposed."

"Ahh." Mandy gave her a look. Amber had her arms crossed and was watching Katie in a way that probably proved the girl had mind-reading abilities.

"You two came over for gossip, didn't you?"

Mandy shrugged, unfazed. "It's Blueberry Springs. It's what we do. And this was simply too good to pass up. You and *him*?" She grinned and popped a square of Angelica's shortbread into her mouth. Her lips turned down as she tasted the undercooked flour and butter mashed together and called a cookie.

"She tried to copy your recipe this year." Katie tried not to be too pleased that Mandy had got that goo all the way into her mouth without warning.

Mandy spit the shortbread into a napkin decorated with snowflakes. "Did she forget to bake them?"

Amber took one. "You're so fussy. They look fine." She chewed, frowned, and reached for a napkin.

Katie checked to make sure her family was still downstairs with Nash, and whispered, "Do people really think Nash asked me to marry him?"

Mandy slid her a sly smile. "Is he the reason your lipstick is all over your face?"

Katie wiped her face with the damp towel.

"Good luck. I saw you buying that never-come-off stuff, which is evil. It sticks everywhere but your lips."

"Now you tell me."

"Hey, you were single. What harm could come to you?"

Katie grumbled and headed back to the kitchen, the friends following her.

"Nash!" Mandy threw up her hands in joy as she spotted the man at the top of the basement stairs. She added a slight sashay to her hips, as she did whenever she saw a man she liked and knew would never challenge the we're-just-friends balance she always created with guys. Without apparent effort she became one of them. Beautiful and feisty, but just one of the guys. Katie wished she could figure that out.

"Mandy, how are you?" Nash gave her an affectionate squeeze

that made Katie's innards feel as though he was squeezing her instead. And not in a good way.

"Missing you." She gave him a harmless, flirty wink.

Jealousy swirled into fury within Katie and she turned to plunge her hands in the lukewarm dishwater.

Okay, she cared.

She liked him.

A lot.

Wanted to date him.

Didn't want him to leave Blueberry Springs.

Big deal.

She could survive that.

"I'm Amber."

"Nash Leham, pleasure to meet you."

Chills swam down Katie's back. He had such a great voice. Low, smooth. Yumalicious.

But he was leaving. Leaving her. If she chose him, she'd be choosing to leave Blueberry Springs forever.

She turned, and her family, who had joined Nash in the kitchen, stilled as though they'd all been touched in a game of freeze tag. "Are you leaving town?" Katie asked him, her heart thundering in her chest.

"Want me out of here?" Nash retorted playfully.

"Not funny."

"I hear Dr. Nesbit is retiring," Amber said, helping herself to eggnog. "If you're asking him to move in with you."

"I have missed Blueberry Springs," Nash said, as though testing the idea. "It might be nice to move back."

"Really?" Beth squealed, grabbing his arm. Oz shot Nash a glare and subtly angled himself between his wife and the man. Katie wished he'd remind his wife who she was married to.

"It's a thought." Nash kept his eyes trained on Katie. "But I'm not sure. I may stay in the city for a while, too."

"I mean, it would be weird if you moved back." Beth blinked

rapidly a few times. "But this isn't about me. It's about you finally finding your mate, so I can get over any weirdness." She beamed and threw up her hands. "Already am."

"What? I think I missed something." Mandy squinted at Beth.

"They'd make an *amazing* couple." She gestured to Nash and Katie.

"Over my dead body," Oz said, at the same as Harvey said, "I agree."

Harvey slung an arm around Katie. "Best medical team in the world. I mean, look at me. Hardly any pain!"

Katie gently moved her father to a chair and forced him to sit. "If you don't take it easy, you'll be black-and-blue and miserable tomorrow."

"Not that different from usual then?" Angelica asked, crossing her arms.

"Anyway, I'm leaving Blueberry Springs," Katie said quietly. "I've decided."

"What?" The room rang with surprised voices all rising to be heard.

"Katie's not staying in nursing," Nash announced calmly. "She's seeking a new career."

"This is Christmas, not April Fool's!" Her father's face was a dangerous red. Katie went to settle him again.

"Are you trying to give him a heart attack?" her mother asked.

"I already told you I'm quitting, Dad."

"You can't just drop a bomb like this," Oz said, his voice tight.

"I thought it was all a joke," Angelica murmured.

"What are you doing to her?" Oz said, confronting Nash. "Why don't you convince my mother to divorce my father while you're at it? Maybe convince my son that I suck as a father? Huh?" He gave Nash a shove.

Mandy was between the men in a flash. "Hey, cool it. We should all get a chance at following our hearts."

Oz leveled a finger at Nash. "He is *not* her heart!"

"So you can follow your dreams, but I can't?" Katie blinked back tears and poked her brother in the chest. "Why? Because I'm a daughter and have to do whatever everyone wants, and be the good girl? The perfect one? The one who doesn't get to do what she prefers because everyone else wants someone to take care of them in their old age? Is that it?"

She burst into tears, furious at herself for crying. Nash was at her side, his arms wrapped around her, in an instant. He felt great. Too great. She pushed at him. "I'm mad at you."

"And I'll be mad if you don't seize your chance to be you, Katie," he said, not allowing her to push him away.

"Okay," Mandy said, a soothing voice among all the squabbling. "Enough. Katie wants to be a decorator. It's obvious that is her calling, if we take a moment to think about all she's done for family and friends over the past few years. She's not going to be able to do both careers. Nursing served its purpose for her and now it is time to move on. So get over it. This is her life. She's the one who gets to live it."

Her family stared at anything and everything other than Katie and Mandy. All except Oz, who was listening to Mandy--really listening. Beth smacked her husband in the chest and he finally looked away.

"Mandy has a point," he said.

"You're with me, remember?" Beth muttered.

"You really don't want to be a nurse?" Harvey asked, his voice thick. Katie shook her head. "But you did want to become a nurse at one point, right?"

"Not really."

Her father's face fell and Katie rushed to his side, hugging him. "But it was a good career, Dad. It's just not me anymore."

He brushed her off. "I can't believe I did this to both of my children." He dropped his face in his hands. "What kind of father am I?"

Katie rubbed his shoulder, taking the seat beside him as Beth began guiding everyone into the dining room. "Let's have dessert so Angelica doesn't get left with all this food," she said.

"You are a great dad," Katie whispered. His shoulders shook. "Dad, really. You wanted what was best for us. Wanted real careers. You didn't want me to be waiting tables all my life, or stocking shelves. You knew that would drive me batty. I need to be in charge. And you helped me get a career that kept me satisfied for years. I don't mind helping people as a nurse, it's just not my passion. You know?"

He gazed at her through his hands, eyes red. "Did I really do okay by you?"

She hugged him tightly. "Of course you did. Do you think I'd let you do any different?"

He gave a thin laugh. "Then why didn't you tell me you didn't want to become a nurse?"

"Because I didn't have anything better in mind."

"How long have you wanted this change?"

Katie sighed. "A few years."

"Why didn't you tell me?"

"You're so proud of me." Katie's own eyes filled with tears. "And what if you're not when I become someone else?"

"You'll still be my daughter, my Katie, and I'll always be immensely proud of you. Always." He placed his hand over hers. "No matter what you do with your life." He tipped his head toward the dining room. "Or who you marry."

"A little ahead of yourself, Dad." But, oddly enough, not ahead of her imagination.

7

So now what was she going to do?

Amber and Mandy had left after a few eggnogs, and Katie's family had called it a night. Beth and Oz took Benji upstairs to stay in Oz's old bedroom rather than stomp through the snow back to their own home, since they would be helping Angelica first thing in the morning, anyway. Which made Katie think they were up to something. Something such as keeping an eye on her and Nash, who were the only ones still up in the living room.

Katie now had her father's blessing not only to toss off the career he'd helped her afford, but to pursue the man who had, up until two days ago, been her arch enemy.

She gazed at the cold fireplace, its bricks blackened from when Oz forgot to open the flue once when they were kids. She half wondered if jolly ol' Saint Nick had given her a gift tonight. A change in plans, a life.

Or maybe it was Nash. Maybe it was him giving her a gift. She leaned into him with a shoulder bump. He smiled and lifted his arm to draw her in.

"So," he began, "I know it's been a big day and all, but I was wondering...did you really decide to move to the city and work for Monica?"

Katie stopped herself from blurting out a defensive rejection.

"She'd pay me, right?"

He nodded.

It was such a risk. No matter how she looked at the situation, it would mean a pay cut. No medical insurance or benefits. No retirement fund. She'd have to move to the city and away from everyone. What if she sucked at it? What if in the real world she didn't have an eye for decorating? And when she was ready to come home, was Blueberry Springs big enough or cosmopolitan enough to support a decorating business? Who would want to pay her for choosing paint colors? Probably nobody.

"I don't really have a choice, do I?"

"There's always a choice."

She laughed. "Right. If I backtrack on what I said today I'll get laughed out of town for being a big chicken." And if she didn't move to the city, would anything further happen between her and Nash?

"Katie?" Nash played with a strand of her hair that had escaped her ponytail.

"Yeah?"

"You wouldn't have told Mary Alice--someone you knew would tell everyone--if you didn't truly want to do this."

Darn smarty-pants. How many psychology courses had he taken in his time?

He reached down beside the couch and handed Katie a small box wrapped in gold foil. The paper was folded so neatly, so crisply, that she knew he had done it himself.

"For me? Thank you."

She tugged at the green velvet bow, then unwrapped the gift. It was a beautiful antique snow globe, unlike any she'd ever seen. Beautiful polished wood for its base, the flakes inside delicate... In the middle was a couple on skates, embracing.

"Nash, it's gorgeous." She could barely breathe. The gift was so extraordinary and unexpected. She threw her arms around him in a quick hug, loving the way his body fit just right against hers. "Thank you."

"You're welcome." His cheeks were pink. "I wasn't sure what you had in your collection, so I figured an antique was likely a safe bet."

"It is. It's amazing. One of a kind." Like Nash. She shifted to face him, honored that he remembered that she had a snow globe collection. "Would you really take Dr. Nesbit's job? Maybe we could live in Blueberry Springs when I'm done in the city. We could move back together."

"Are you asking me to marry you, Katie Reiter?"

She laughed and snuggled against his side, feeling warm and comfortable. "Okay, so I move a little fast sometimes, but yeah. Maybe. One day. If we decide we actually like each other."

He tipped her chin up to kiss her. "I happen to like fast. And I already know I like you."

"Good," she said, then kissed him back. Nash was all the things she wanted in a man. And more. Much more than what she'd ever dreamed of having.

But could she really have him? Could she have it all? Her heart beat fast and hard. So much was unknown, but instead of scaring her, it made her excited--especially knowing that Nash might be there, too.

She was ready, for the first time in her life, to not overthink things and simply start walking forward to see what happened.

She'd had a big plan with nursing and Will, and had stayed with it because she'd feared there was nothing else out there for her. She'd believed Will was her one chance at happiness and marriage.

Now she knew better.

She kissed Nash on the lips and smiled. "Thank you, Nash. You're the best thing that has happened to me in a long time."

"Anything for you, Katie bear."

"Did you really just call me that?"

"Whatever it takes to get you to the city with me, until we are both ready to come back to Blueberry Springs."

"Moving rather fast, aren't you?"

"I told you I like fast. Are you going to have a problem with that?"

She swung around so she was straddling his lap. "Not at all."

"I know what I want, Katie. I want to date you. You are the reason I came back to Blueberry Springs. I could have spent the days off with my parents, so remember that if you ever doubt me and my intentions. I couldn't get you--" he clutched her chin, ensuring she was listening, his voice gentle, yet demanding "--out of my mind."

Katie paused, her chest tight with emotion. She rested a hand in the dip below his shoulder. She loved this man. And not just because he was saying things she'd always longed to hear. "Thank you for joining my family for the holidays."

"I'd like to again next year."

Katie pushed herself to standing. She needed to get her brain on track. When she was this close to him, everything he said sounded good. Easy. She let out a laugh. "For once I am thinking of not planning my life, and here you are, planning it. Believe it or not, you might be moving too fast for me, Nash Leham."

KATIE SLIPPED INTO THE KITCHEN, the light above the stove casting a quiet glow over the room. A shot of something strong would be nice to settle her nerves right about now.

A figure moved at the table. Beth.

"Can't sleep?" Katie asked, digging through the cupboard for peppermint schnapps.

"I'm pregnant, so of course not. It's like my body is telling me to get used to it. Driving me crazy."

Katie sat with her friend, who was clutching a cup of hot chocolate.

"Remember when you lived with Nash and his pretentious coffeemaker?"

Beth smiled wanly.

Katie had been angry with her for living that high on the hog with Nash. But mostly it was misdirected anger at her friend for changing. For daring to want something more from her life and for being brave enough to take it. For knowing she deserved to be happy, and claiming it any way she could.

How silly and immature Katie had been.

"So? Are you going back to Dakota with him?" Beth asked, breaking the peaceful, middle-of-the-night silence.

"I am going to talk to his friend who is a decorator, but I'm not…I'm not moving in with him, if that's what you are asking."

"He's a good man."

Katie nodded. "I know."

Beth scrunched her big brown eyes shut, let out a breath, then opened them again. "You should date him. Really."

"Is this Pregnant Beth talking or Whatever is Good for My BFF talking?"

Beth let out a tinkling laugh. "Everyone but your pigheaded brother agrees you two are a good fit."

"Won't it be weird?" To know that her best friend had been with the man who held her heart. Would Katie ever be able to let the twinges of jealousy go?

"We dated some of the same guys in high school."

"Yeah, because there was no selection. You had to share men and then stay friends with them after dumping their sorry selves, because there was nobody else in town."

"Is that why you stayed with Will for so long? Lack of selection?"

"Lack of understanding myself, too."

"You need to do this, Katie." Beth reached across the table. "The two of you are a better fit than we ever were. He came into my life for a reason, but it wasn't to marry him. Maybe he's come into your life for a bigger, longer-term reason."

"You're putting the cart before the horse here, don't you think?"

Everyone was moving so darn fast!

"Shh. Quit fighting. You're finally getting what you want."

"What if it's wrong?" Katie whispered. "What if I am on the rebound? What if…" She tried to think of more excuses. None were coming.

"What if you are being a big chicken and need to follow your heart? You were never scared with Will, and you want to know why? Because you always knew he wasn't ever going to break your heart. And you know why?"

Fierce Beth had come to town. "Why?" Katie asked in a feeble voice.

"Because you never loved him! He can't break your heart if he doesn't have access to it."

Katie sat back, the news hitting her so hard she had trouble breathing.

"Now go in there and tell Nash you love him. That you can't live without him and you want to have hot monkey sex with him." Beth swiped at her damp eyes.

"Beth? I think the hormones might be controlling the mother ship."

Her friend slammed a fist on the table, her cheeks pink. "Shut up and claim him already!"

So this was it.

Nash was heading back to the city. Blueberry Springs had been dug out overnight and the roads were open once again.

The day felt like a big letdown. The holidays were officially over. All that prep and then boom. Celebration finished. Life resumed as normal.

Only this time life was no longer normal. It was as though Katie had finally received the pony she'd been wishing for. She wasn't left sitting by the tree among the shredded wrappings, wondering why Santa had bypassed her once again.

She had the pony and, as a result, her whole world had opened up. All she had to do was walk out into the yard and claim it.

Claim her new career. Claim the man she'd carefully sidestepped all last night while she mulled over Beth's advice, her own feelings, his words.

It was time to step out of her pre-pony days and become the girl she'd always dreamed of being.

She didn't need a life plan; she was living it this time. Eyes open. Arms out wide. Ready to grab it all.

Nash was hers. She'd known it in her heart as soon as her eyes had opened this morning. The hollow spot within her had been filled and she couldn't wait to see him.

And right now, that was all that mattered.

Stretching, Katie walked to the living room's bay window and took in the snowy scene. Her mother's yard decorations were still buried under massive drifts, the street invisible behind the piles of snow the plows had left. In a while, Katie would go home to her basement suite and call Nash's friend Monica, then start figuring out what she needed to take with her to the city. But first she was going to help her mother put on the best post-Christmas buffet in the history of the Reiter household. A little something to try and help stretch out the holidays for her mom.

As Katie turned from the window, something caught her eye. What was that? It looked like the roof of a silver BMW squirreling its way to a stop in front of the house.

She knew only one person who drove a Beemer. She flung open the front door, slipping into her father's winter boots on her way out. She clunked up to the car, sliding to a halt as the driver's door opened.

"Nash!"

He wrapped her in his arms, breathing her in as if they hadn't seen each other in months. "Katie."

Her name sounded amazing tumbling out of his rumbly chest, with her body clutched against his.

"I missed you already." She laughed, tipping her head up to smile at him. His nose was red from the cold. "You are going to have to buy a more rugged vehicle if you move back, you know. One with a good heater."

"Maybe you can keep me warm." He kissed her in a way that made the need for a winter coat unnecessary. "I missed you, too," he murmured, his lips warm against hers. She sagged into him, allowing his strength to support them both.

"I love you." She blinked and took a sharp breath. She hadn't meant to say that.

But it felt right. Scary, it was so right.

"Good." He squeezed her against him, his voice thick with emotion. While he seemed so strong, possibly he needed someone like her in his life. Someone who was strong enough to be his anchor. And when it came to anchors, not just anyone would do. But she would.

She smiled, knowing she would one day be the woman he came home to. The woman who, starting now, would hold him strong against the current.

"I love you, Katie Reiter," he whispered in her ear. "Be mine."

"It's not Valentine's Day, silly man," she teased, her eyes filling with gratitude and love.

"I know, but I want you today and every day until then. And then beyond. Much beyond." He held her face so he could meet her eyes. "Can you handle that?"

"Challenge accepted, Nash Leham. Challenge gladly and wholeheartedly accepted."

* * *

Thank you for reading EGGNOG AND CANDY CANES. I hope you adored Katie and Nash. What happens next in Blueberry Springs? Valentine's Day! Proposals are made. Promises are broken. Relationships are redeemed. Fall in love with these short stories, and catch up with your favorite Blueberry Springs characters in the mini anthology SWEET TREATS. Here's a little sneak peek of what's to come…

Be my Valentine, Blueberry Springs.

Story 1: One new job. One chance to prove herself. And one crush on the man she most definitely shouldn't.

Will Nicola Samuels truly be immune to the holiday? Or will Cupid strike and ruin it all?

Story 2: One happy couple. One friend with a not-so-secret crush. One Valentine's Day that could change it all.

When Amber's boyfriend gets held up in the city, her best friend Scott Malone picks up his slack. But will Scott's good intentions be noticed for what they truly are? Or will Cupid's arrow miss his target?

Story 3: One woman. One man. One question.

Mandy is struggling to expand her new restaurant in hopes of becoming more financially secure, but she doesn't know what to do when Frankie asks for the one thing she doesn't have— more time to spend with him… Will Mandy find a way to have her cake and eat it too?

Find SWEET TREATS in your favorite bookstore!

"Funny, romantic, enjoyable and lively Blueberry Springs. What a fun community to live in!!!" —Reader review.

SIGN UP FOR Jean's newsletter to stay in the know about deals, new books and more! www.jeanoram.com/signup

* * *

Have you fallen in love with Blueberry Springs? Catch up with your friends and their adventures in the complete Blueberry Springs series:

Book 1: Whiskey and Gumdrops (Mandy & Frankie)

Book 2: Rum and Raindrops (Jen & Rob)

Book 3. Eggnog and Candy Canes (Katie & Nash)

Book 4: Sweet Treats (3 short stories—Mandy, Amber, & Nicola)

Book 5: Vodka and Chocolate Drops (Amber & Scott)

Book 6: Tequila and Candy Drops (Nicola & Todd)

Companion Novel: Champagne and Lemon Drops (Beth & Oz)

www.ingramcontent.com/pod-product-compliance
Lightning Source LLC
Chambersburg PA
CBHW061457210726

48287CB00007B/2550